A SOUND OF TRUMPETS

by the same author

THE HILL OF THE RED FOX
RIBBON OF FIRE

available as Canongate Kelpies

A SOUND
OF TRUMPETS

Allan
Campbell McLean

CANONGATE · KELPIES

First published 1967 by Collins, London
First published in Kelpies 1985

Copyright © 1966 Allan Campbell McLean.

Cover illustration by Jill Downie

Printed in Great Britain
by Cox & Wyman Ltd, Reading, Berkshire

ISBN 0 86241 095 9

*The publishers acknowledge the financial assistance
of the Scottish Arts Council in the
publication of this volume*

CANONGATE PUBLISHING LTD
17 JEFFREY STREET, EDINBURGH EH1 1DR

for
Jeff, Sandra, and Ian

I

He was dying, that was a sure thing.

The thick peat reek in the room dimmed the guttering oil lamp, but the flames from the splinters of bog fir I had cast on the glowing peats lit the dark recess in the wall where he lay on a pallet of fresh straw. His face looked wasted. The skin was drawn tight over the bones, grey and withered, glazed with a sickly sweat. His eyes were open, but he was too far gone in the fever to know where he was or who was about him.

There had been a strong breeze of wind blowing all day. With the tide on the flood, it had backed to the north and now it was raging near gale force. It swept across the high moorland at the back of the house and came screaming down around the drystone walls, threatening to pluck the heather-roped thatch from the roof. Whenever there was a lull between gusts, the thunder of the surf crashing on the shore was suddenly loud in the room.

He stirred every time the storm slackened, twisting his head from side to side, his left hand searching for the stump in his empty shirt-sleeve. Groans and terrible swears spilled from his lips. A thin line of spittle trickled down his chin into his beard and the sweat ran free.

I knew fine he was thinking the boom of the surf was the roar of the Russian cannon at Sebastopol. He was living again the loss of his right arm in the war, not seeing me at all—frozen by the wall-bed in an agony of fear—his eyes fixed on a battlefield in the Crimea, and it near thirty years since the shot was fired that destroyed his arm.

He had the fever bad, our father.

A week last Thursday—just nine days ago—he had been in great form, hurrying into his good Sabbath clothes long before the first light of dawn had flushed the eastern sky above the hills of Wester Ross. As I laced his best boots for him, the words tumbled out in full spate.

"It will be a great meeting, *'ille*," he said, eager as a boy making ready for his first horse fair. "There was never the like in this place, you may be sure o' that. They are coming from all over, great speakers, the best just—Members o' Parliament and Ministers o' the Gospel some of them. They say a Duncan MacGregor is to be there—a minister and a great preacher the same one—and himself all the way from Chicago in America. His father was a poor crofter from Glenshiel way, driven out by a rag of a laird in '35 and shipped to America in the *Cherokee*. A floating coffin just, the *Cherokee*. They say she was 107 days out of Liverpool before they sighted Boston. And near all the four hundred emigrants aboard buried at sea before the voyage was half done. They perished o' ship-fever, poor souls, the conditions were that bad. But Duncan MacGregor's father was spared, and his son is to be here to-day speaking for the Scottish Land League of America—and himself a minister! A pity we hadn't more ministers o' his stamp in this place. Ach, well, some o' them may take strength when they see the crowd that is out to-day, and the big men we have speaking up for our rights."

He had gone off with all the men of our township and all the townships around the place, and to see the blithe step they had on them you would not have believed there

8

was seventeen miles of rough heath and moorland track between themselves and Portree.

Our men were met on the road out of Portree by all the men of that village, with three pipers at their head and young folk bearing banners; and they were joined in the big market square, where the horse fairs are held, by the men of Dunvegan and the men of Waternish and the men of The Braes. The like of that gathering had never been seen before. Even the old men said so, and it is a wonder beyond measure when the old men will admit to anything topping the great days of their perished youth.

I would have gone with my father but the *cailleach* took to her bed the day before, and someone had to see to the cattle. Now that she was thirteen, my sister Mairi was working away all week at the Lodge, where the gentry stayed for the fishing and the shooting, and Mairi only got home every fourth Sabbath. That left little Seoras, eight years old and good enough as a herd, but a poor hand at the milking.

I mind well how our mother did not rise from her bed that day until it was dark, and far too late for me to think of making for Portree. From the way she bustled around— busying herself straight off making girdle scones and preparing a pot of broth—it was clear that whatever ailed her had been banished wonderful swift with the coming of night. She even sang to herself, and it was not often she was in the mood for singing, the *cailleach*.

But as the night wore on, and there was no sign of our father, the singing gave way to a silent fury of work; and when all the work of the house was done she could not contain herself on her birch-bough stool by the fire. She was for ever prowling to the door and peering out into the dark of the night and shaking her head and tutting to herself, all the lines—and she had gathered many a deep-grooved line in the course of the years, our mother—in her sharp face drooping in disapproval, putting me in mind of her father, the old *Ceistear*, who always looked as if the Day of Judgment was about to dawn, and himself certain sure there would be scant joy in it for the rest of us.

About midnight, the wind got up; a wild, wet wind from the south, bringing the rainclouds down upon us. *Dhia*, how it rained! It dripped through the hole in the thatch that served as a chimney, hissing and sizzling on the big iron pot and exploding in the red embers of the fire. The wind flung the rain about the house, beating against the door, driving under the narrow gap and spreading black on the earthen floor.

The *cailleach* hunched her shoulders, a sure sign she was not pleased. "That man is not wise," she said, "out on the moor at this time o' night and the rain coming down something terrible. He should have had sense and stayed snug at home like you, Alasdair."

"Supposing you had not taken to your bed, I would have been out along with him," I reminded her, stung to anger by the thought of what I had missed.

She gave me a sharp look, but all she said was: "Well, it is a blessing you are in the dry. The laird will be back at the end o' this month, and then it is you for the school in Edinburgh."

She was fitting fresh peats into the crumbling shell of the fire under the big iron pot where the broth was cooking, and she took her time about it, as if there was something precious in the glowing heart of the fire that she did not want to disturb. I knew her well enough to know that she was seeing rosy pictures in the red embers; pictures of me in Edinburgh at a school where English was spoken all the time, where there was never a whisper of Gaelic to soil the air, not even in the lavatory far from the ears of the masters; pictures of myself secure in an office job on the laird's estate, perhaps even becoming factor through time, and rising to be a big man in the place.

She brushed a wisp of grey hair out of her eyes. "It would not do for you to be laid up in bed, Alasdair," she said, in a voice grown soft all of a sudden, "and the laird expecting you to be ready for off."

"I am ready," I said, although in truth I was not. "But I am not so sure about the laird."

"How not?" she demanded angrily. "You had the letter from Miss Fiona, didn't you? Good grief, it is not a week since it came wi' the mail. Are you after forgetting the letter?"

I was not likely to be forgetting it, seeing it was the one and only letter that had ever come to me at home in all my born days—and I said as much to her.

"Well, then, is the laird's daughter telling lies when she says her father will be back in Skye the last day in September? —and herself to be travelling along with him, and fair delighted by her way of it? That is what you read in the letter. I mind every word of it, boy—every word, mind."

"The laird went off to England last May," I said, fighting to keep my voice down, and the fight lost before I was right started, "and the word was he would be back in June with a new factor to fix fair rents and see that we got back our land that was taken from us and given to the tacksman. Then it was July he was to be back, and then August. But the laird has still to show face, and there has been no word of a new factor or fair rents or the return of the land that was taken from us. Maybe the laird has been listening to the talk of the English lairds, and maybe that talk has made dust of all his fine promises, and that is why he is staying away from the place."

She was not slow in getting up off her low birch-bough stool, and I am telling you she had some rage on her. Seoras was sleeping in a corner of the wooden bench, and she let out such a bark he woke in a fright.

"You are as bad as your father," she cried. "What do you know of the gentry and their ways? Do you suppose the laird has nothing better to do than leap to the bidding of Iain Beag and Eachunn Ruadh and Coinneach the Piper and the like, a pack of idle wastrels as sure as I am here? Let me tell you, boy, the laird has more to do with his time than that. You have no idea, boy, no idea. I know the gentry and their ways. *I know them!* Before I ever came to this." She spread her arms wide, taking in the lime-washed, drystone walls; the peat fire, set cosy in the centre of the earthen floor; the big iron soup pot that hung secure on its smoke-grimed chain from the tar-black roof beams; the rough deal table with the squint leg; the spinning-wheel in the corner beyond the bench; the wall-bed, hidden by a ragged blanket curtain, where I slept with Seoras: her outspread arms took them all in, and the sight of them did not please her over-much, if the look she cast around was anything to go by—"I was in service for years in many a Big House for the gentry, not only in this place but on the mainland, too. I tell you, boy, you have no idea. The gentry are on the go every single minute of the day what with fishing and shooting and many a queer sport I don't even mind the name of, and big dinners and balls galore, and changing their clothes for this and that, and dressing special every night in life before they sit in to the table and take a bite. It is a wonder to me the laird ever has time to be thinking o'——"

She wanted a bad word, I knew that fine, but not one bad enough to disturb the shade of her father, the old *Ceistear*, and I got in fast with: "The like of us?"

"The like o' the idlers in this place," she countered, "who are for ever making lies and putting folk against their betters wi' their wicked talk. Talk never filled a meal chest yet, let me tell you. In my father's days there was none o' this nonsense. Folk attended to their work and counted their blessings and respected their superiors and there was peace in the place."

"Well, they are wiser now," I said.

"Wise, did you say?" She fairly spat the words at me. "It is yourself is not wise, boy. The laird is pleased to smile upon you and lift you above your fellows with a right schooling in Edinburgh and a start on the estate, and all because you brought word that Miss Fiona had come off her horse and was hurt. The laird has been too good to you, that is the truth as I am here. Many's the one would have had you put to the jail seeing the way you carried on—you and that Lachlann Ban. It is a blessing the same one is clear o' the place and on his way to America. He will find trouble enough there, I would not wonder. But now that he is gone I am telling you this: you will close your ears to the wicked talk of idlers, and as long as I am mistress o' this house you will not make mock o' the laird, or I will take a stick to your back and beat sense into you, stubborn an' all as you are."

It was lack of breath that stopped her, or she would have gone on for long enough. As she paused, flushed and hot-eyed, we both heard the singing. Men's voices, sounding out above the noise of the wind and the rain, loud and free of care, threaded with laughter that bubbled out like a hard-boiling pot that cannot be contained.

By the time the *cailleach* had the door open our father was into the room, a right crowd at his back, and that was the end of the strife.

Wet? They were that wet you would think they had newly climbed out of the deepest pool on the river. Iain Beag was without a bonnet, his black hair plastered to his head like the glistening coat of a seal, and the face of every one of them was whipped raw by the wind and the rain. But every single one of them was in great form.

The *cailleach* took our father's sodden topcoat and bonnet, her nose giving a twitch as she sniffed the whisky on his breath. His trousers were black with rain, and she hissed at him to get them off, but he sat down on the bench, never heeding, taking Seoras on his knee, and turning to Coinneach the Piper and Iain Beag and Colla the smith and Eachunn Ruadh, and the others crowding in behind them, crying: "Well, boys, was it not a great meeting? The best ever just!"

There was a loud chorus of assent, flowing as strong as a flood-tide, with little eddying bursts of talk filling every corner of the room.

And then, to me: "A pity you were not along with us, Alasdair. It was great altogether."

And to the others: "You mind the minister, the one with the queer Gaelic? I don't mind his name. A stranger to me; I never laid eyes on the man in my life. They were saying he was from Golspie. Ach, he was good, the minister."

He rose to his feet, Seoras held firm in his strong left arm. Speaking loud and clear in the queerest Gaelic I ever heard, he said: "Some people say we are making too much noise. But how were the walls of Jericho laid in the dust? By a great noise of trumpets. We have the command, 'Ask and ye shall receive,' and I say to you we must thunder, thunder, thunder at the doors of the lairds until they meet the just demands of the people."

He sat down suddenly on the bench, clutching Seoras to him, the rest of them shouting in great glee: "Aye, right enough. That was the Golspie minister to the life." He was good at the mimicking, our father.

Coinneach the Piper passed round a jug of whisky, and there was such a babble of talk not one of them heard the *cailleach* saying there was a bowl of broth and a girdle scone for all who fancied a bite. But she sat quiet on her stool, knowing well enough that the time would come when they would take heed of the steaming pot of broth and tease her for keeping it back from them. And I will say this for her: although she was against strong drink something terrible, she was not the one to interfere in the ways of men, not like her father, the old *Ceistear*, who would have smashed the jugs with his stick, and driven the whole crowd of them out into the night—supposing they had ever had the nerve to face him in the first place.

Iain Beag produced his melodeon from its sail-cloth wrapping, and what with tunes on the melodeon; and a wild *port-a-beul* from Eachunn Ruadh that had big Colla the smith leaping in the dance, wonderful nimble and dainty in the steps, for all his heavy tackety boots, and everyone's feet—even the *cailleach's*—drumming out the blood-heating rhythm on the earthen floor; and songs coming thick and fast: well, I am telling you, I never saw a *ceilidh* hasten to the boil so quick. Indeed, they were all that eager to see justice done to the great songs the bards had made in olden times that one man was no sooner done singing than another was starting anew.

The *ceilidh* was going on long after I carried the sleeping

Seoras to bed, and it showed no signs of slackening when I got in beside him, hours later. I woke once, hearing Colla the smith's deep, rumbling laugh, and at the back of that familiar, belly-heaving laugh I mind there came the thin crow of a cockerel. After that, I slept like a dead thing. The sun was past the meridian before I opened my eyes again.

The next day our father never rose from his bed. The following day he was sweating bad in the grip of the fever. The third day we got fresh straw for the pallet that Seoras and I shared, and the *cailleach* and I half dragged, half carried him into the wall-bed so that he could be near the fire.

That was six days ago, and he had failed something terrible since then.

"Away to bed, boy," the *cailleach* said.

I had forgotten she was there, crouched low on the birch-bough stool by the fire, she had been that quiet.

"I will wait a whiley yet," I said, and sat down on the bench.

"Away to your bed," she repeated, but there was no bite in her voice. Her shadowed, deep-sunk eyes never lifted from the fire.

"Iain should be back any time now," I said.

She nodded.

Iain Beag had gone to Uig with the doctor in his gig to fetch medicine for the *bodach*. He was a hardy man, Iain Beag, but many a thing could have happened to him on the long walk home from the doctor's house in Uig. I know I would not have fancied the lonely miles over the hill, with the wind screaming like a thousand unleashed demons as it tore through the cleft of the high pass that led down to the plain below and our township. It was the sort of night when you would think twice before going the length of the stackyard, if you were wise.

"He is a great walker, Iain," I said. "You may be sure there is not a man in the place could make better time than Iain Beag."

She did not speak. We sat in silence, if you could call it silence with the frantic howl of the gale beating about the house, and the roaring *boom* . . . *boom* . . . *boom* of the surf pounding on the shore.

There would be plenty driftwood to be lifted in the morning, there always was after a northerly gale, but the corn would be flat, that was a sure thing. And there would be one reaping hook the less at the lifting of the corn this harvest—that was a sure thing, too.

The thought was like ashes in my mouth; the taste of death itself could not be more bitter. It was in me to run to the bed to see if he had stopped breathing, but I sat tight on the bench, motionless as the frozen figure of the *cailleach*, crouched by the fire.

We never heard Iain Beag fumbling for the latch, such was the noise of the storm. The wind roared in as the door flew open, very near lifting the roof entire. The lamp went out. Sparks flurried across the earthen floor as the fire scattered. The *cailleach* gave one strangled screech and sprang to her feet.

It took the two of us to force the door shut against the strength of the wind. Iain Beag groped his way to the bench. He slumped down, fairly gasping for air he was that spent.

I tossed some splinters of bog fir on the fire. The flickering flames cast strange shadows on the walls, and lit the face of Iain Beag, a face that lathered in sweat you would have thought he had been swinging a hammer over the raging heat of the forge in Colla's smithy.

That did not surprise me. But there was something else— a queer excitement about him, and himself not the man to be easily stirred, shrugging off with his quick laugh many a thing that would have put most men up to high doh.

I had crossed to the bench and was sitting beside him when he got his tongue working. "Bad news," he panted, spitting the words out in quick, breathless bursts. "They got word . . . on the telegraph . . . in Uig. The laird is dead."

2

Just ten days after Iain Beag had brought word of the death of the laird our father was out of bed, the fever conquered, and sitting in his usual place on the bench. That night, everything about the house was the way it had always been; the smoke of many pipes mingling with the slow drift of the peat reek; the air fairly crackling with talk there were that many tongues on the go—and no man laying off his chest more than the *bodach*.

I could not but marvel when I gazed upon him—so small and spare, so bent about the shoulders, so deeply lined in the face, the beard on him as grey as the coat of an old badger—that he was alive still. I wondered what Miss Fiona was thinking, and her father dead. The laird had been a man in the middle years, not a single speck of grey in the raven black of his hair and beard, the lineaments of power marked strong upon his countenance, such power that he could have had doctors galore come running at the lift of a finger. I could not think of him as dead, although I was eager enough to accept the fact that his plans for me had perished as surely as the flame of a candle is snuffed by the meeting of a finger and thumb.

It is queer how ideas take root in a body or wither, much as seed will quicken with life or lie barren, depending on the state of the ground. When I was sick with the rheumatic fever and the laird came to see me in the big Glasgow hospital and told me of his plans—how I was to get special lessons from the *Maighstir* during the summer, and then make off to Edinburgh for a right schooling so that I would be fitted for a place in the factor's office on the estate—I never doubted that it would be so, or questioned the wisdom of becoming more expert in the use of a pen than the *cas-chrom*.

But once I got clear of the hospital in May, and breathed again the air of our island, and wandered barefoot the moors and hills, and felt the strength surging back into my limbs, so that I could run and leap with scarce a quickened breath the way I had always done: why, the very notion of going to a strange school in a strange city on the mainland was shed entire.

As the summer sped by, and the reaping hooks were taken out and given a fine edge on the stone ready for the ripening harvest, the feeling grew within me that the Edinburgh jaunt would never come to pass. Indeed, I often wondered what I was doing wasting time taking lessons from the *Maighstir* when I could have been carting home peats or gathering sheep for the clipping fank or trying a pool on the river for a salmon like all the others of my age.

So you can see why it was that the news of the death of the laird had a special meaning for me. Every man in the place was in fear wondering what like a man our new master would be, knowing fine it would be a queer laird who would not seek to squeeze from us the last penny owing in rent, but, in truth, I was not worrying. A new laird meant the certain surety that there would be no schooling in Edinburgh for me, and I would be free to make my own way among my own people with no stranger to single me out from the many and place me at a distance from my own.

Not that the *cailleach* ever harboured such thoughts. She was certain sure that the laird would have left word on what was to be done for me, and that his instructions would be carried out to the letter by obedient servants.

Many's the time when we were alone together she would fasten her brooding eyes on me, and say, "Never you fear, Alasdair, word will come from the laird, you may be sure o' that. The gentry always have everything marked down in case they are taken sudden. They are not like us, at all, at all. See you, it is easy enough to depart this world supposing all you possess is a beast or two and a weight o' gear no heavier than the clothes you carry on your back. Your only worry is the saving of your immortal soul. But the gentry are yoked something terrible to worldly affairs. They have that much business on the go, what with lands and houses galore, and gear and the like, and orders about this and that within the family—not just for their children but their children's children—they must make provision from beyond the grave if there is to be peace and order thereafter. That is why they have everything marked down. As sure as fate, we will be hearing from a lawyer man one o' these days, and that will be you off to the school in Edinburgh."

She never lost faith, I will say that for her, although September was spent without her prophecy being fulfilled. Indeed, the harvest was gathered and stacked—if you could call it a harvest seeing the September storms had blackened the corn and beaten it to the ground, making of the lifting a heartache, and no real winter feed there for the cattle when it came to the bit, despite all our labour—and the first snow of October had whitened the high hills of Wester Ross without the least glimmer of hope coming from the south to sustain her.

But my word you should have seen her face the day Mairi raced into the house, clutching a letter fresh from the mail coach, shouting: "A letter for Alasdair! A letter for Alasdair!"

The *cailleach* snatched it out of Mairi's hand. She held it close to her face, squinting at the envelope as if determined to master the art of reading there and then by sheer force of will. Supposing Mairi had uncovered a hoard of gold, the *cailleach* could not have handled it with greater reverence or been slower in passing it on to me.

I sat down on the bench and broke open the envelope and drew out a single sheet of thick white notepaper, edged with black. I never saw the like of that paper, near as thick as board, beautiful to the touch it was that satin smooth in finish. The address was raised up, each letter a separate island standing out sharp and clear:

NORTON MANOR, STOWEY CROSS, SOMERSET

The writing was in Fiona's quick, bold hand.

"Have you lost your tongue, boy?" the *cailleach* snapped, her hands that tightly pressed together you could near feel the bones cracking. "What does the letter say?"

"*Dear Alasdair*," I read. "*The General* (she always called her father 'The General') *is dead. He was thrown by his hunter and died before a doctor could be summoned. I cannot believe he is gone.*

"*My Uncle Randolph is taking me to his home in Ireland. The General's estates in North Britain will be in the hands of his Edinburgh lawyers until I am of age. I have told them of his plans for you. When a factor is appointed it will be for him to see that The General's wishes are carried out.*

> *I am,*
>> *Ever your friend,*
>>> *Fiona Kemball-Denison* "

"It will be the worse for us," our father said, "if we are to be at the mercy o' lawyers—and Edinburgh lawyers at that. The law is working for the landlord, and you may be sure the lawyers will not be idle so long as a penny in rent is owing."

The *cailleach* did not bark or sniff or even cast him a glance. I do not believe she heard a single word. She took the letter out of my hand, that flushed and proud-looking you would have thought she held in her grasp the key to the Kingdom of Heaven.

"Wait you, Alasdair," she crowed, "once the factor is here that is you for off, and many a one in this place will be wishing they were in your boots. It will be a great day in this house, I am telling you, when the new factor comes."

He had no sooner stepped down the gangway of the *Clydesdale* as she berthed at the pier in Portree, and climbed into the waiting coach drawn by the laird's four jet-black Highland ponies, than word of his coming sped from mouth to mouth, travelling from township to township with the speed of a heath fire in a dry spring when the old heather flares like tinder and the advancing flames eat up the moor in giant strides. I do not believe the telegraph could have moved faster.

That night our house was packed to the door, but there was not the usual noisy clatter of tongues. The silence hung that heavy you could very near sniff the fear in the air. When Tomas the Elder cleared his throat, and started to speak, his words were that slow in coming, and his countenance so cast down, it was in me to believe we were gathered for a prayer meeting.

"It is a mockery of the people," Tomas cried, "that is what it is, a mockery just. If the laird was living Major

Traill would not be back as factor to oppress us. Good grief, it was the laird himself put the same one away from the place once he got word of the evil that was being done in his name. And now the bold fellow is back to plague us!"

He gazed at the silent, set faces all around, scanning each in turn, and slowly held up his right hand, three stubby fingers stretched wide.

"Three rises in our rents, that was the work o' Major Traill. Three rises in our rents, and all in a handful o' years, lean years at that, bad harvests the most of them, and hard winters every one, the corries thick wi' snow before November was right in, and the stackyards empty before February was done; the cattle that desperate for a bite they would have eaten the rushes off our roofs supposing they could have got near. And what like were the prices we were getting for our beasts? Fine the dealers knew there was not a man in the place dare turn back a beast from the sales we were that short o' feed. So prices were away to nothing, but still an' all the major put up our rents—and took the most of our hill pasture from us, and wanted another rent paid before we could strip a turf from the bogs and cut peats, and money to be handed over for the right to gather whelks from the shore, and drift timber not to be lifted on pain o' the jail—you mind the notice he had up in the shop about it?—drift timber to lie on the rocks waiting the major's pleasure. Well, I'm telling you there is no living for us in this place now that Major Traill is back as factor. We had best make a petition and put it away to the lawyers in Edinburgh, telling how the laird cleared the major out o' the place—and that not a twelvemonth since—and saying we are not for having him back as factor."

Once more Tomas the Elder scanned the faces all around,

24

and once more not a one spoke. I saw the *cailleach's* lips moving as she tutted silently to herself, not pleased to hear a voice raised against those placed in authority over us, not even when the spokesman was a godly man like Tomas the Elder, who spent near all his time on his knees when he was not working, and had never been known to take strong drink.

"That is the truth, as I am here," said Tomas angrily. "It was the laird himself put the major away."

Iain Beag shrugged. "The laird is dead," he said.

My father nodded. "Aye, and the bold major is the very man the lawyers would be seeking for to factor the place. Supposing we were foolish enough to go near them wi' petitions and the like they would be after choking us with their long words—and putting in a fierce charge for every one o' them, I would not wonder. All the lawyers are wanting from the estate is money. The rent collected regular and that is them fair delighted. They are not worrying supposing every widow woman in the place is that hard pressed to find the rent she is eating limpets off the rocks."

"It will come to that for the whole crowd of us, nothing surer," Tomas the Elder said.

"I am not saying you nay, Tomas." My father's steady eyes—eyes that had gazed upon far-off battlefields I would never know—measured every one of them in the room. "I mind Lachlann Ban telling how we would be driven to the shore to live on limpets if the factor had his way of it. I mind Lachlann Ban saying the word o' the factor is the only law in this place, and we would be no better than beasts o' burden until we cleared such a rag of a law from our backs and stood as free men. Lachlann Ban was the wise one."

"Lachlann Ban," they all said, speaking his name on a dying fall, so that it sounded like the fading close of a lament, and there was a stirring among them, as sudden as the first flurry of wind that ruffles the dawn calm. I knew fine that every one of them was seeing in his mind's eye the same picture I had of Lachlann Ban, his face laid open to the bone where the factor had slashed him with his riding crop, advancing on the major, wresting the leather crop from his grasp, and clubbing the bigger man to the ground with his bare fists.[1] Many a one we could have spared to make off to America, but not Lachlann Ban.

"Lachlann Ban was all for putting an end to the rule o' the lairds and the factors," my father went on, "but the most o' you thought you were secure enough seeing the fine promises the laird made. But the laird is dead, poor man, his promises dust, and our new masters will never come near the place, if the factor does his work for them—and he will do that, the same one."

Colla the smith nodded grimly. "And the major is not the man to be slow in starting," he said, "you may be sure o' that."

Neither he was. Next Monday night every man in the place clad in good Sabbath clothes, best boots shining—packed into the new school, tight as herring in a barrel, in answer to the factor's summons. The wooden partition dividing the classrooms had been slid open on its brass runners to make one big room, but even so there was a crowd standing at the back, spilling out into the lobby. I had to perch on an upturned fire pail and peer over their heads before I got a view of what was going on inside. Even so, it would be a wonder if I was allowed to stay there, seeing the black looks

[1] Ribbon of Fire.

I was getting from the four helmeted policemen at the door. And there was another six of them waiting in a wagonette outside the gates of the school, to remind those who might be tempted to dispute the word of the factor that he need only crook his finger to have the law come running.

Mind you, it was comical seeing grown men squeezed into the scholars' desks, and I very nearly burst out laughing at the awful job some of them had trying to struggle to their feet when the factor came in. But one look at Major Traill choked the rising laughter dead in my throat.

He strode in with a right swagger on him, like a conqueror come to survey his assembled captives; a big man, well fleshed, the years of command stamped clear upon his person; a proud man, head held high, cold blue eyes surveying the room without interest, for all the world as if he beheld before him rows of penned cattle, and himself a man with no notion for cattle beasts.

And trotting at his heels, a nervous hand hovering close to the factor's elbow, hoping to make us believe he was the guide and not an obedient follower, came the tall, stooping, terrible thin figure of the *Maighstir*, Mr. Nicolson.

Not that we thought the worse of him for that. The *Maighstir* did not belong to the place, and he had his job to think of, poor man. The factor was chairman of the School Board: one word from him and that was Mr. Nicolson out of his fine new schoolhouse, and down the road, and maybe many a long mile to put behind him before he found its equal.

But there was no excuse for the man who followed the *Maighstir* into the room, smiling his false smile whenever he was sure the factor's eyes were not on him. He *was* one of us, born and bred in the place, and there were those who remembered the day when his father did not possess so much as a poke of meal, and was dependent on the charity of his neighbours for the means of life. But it was changed days now for that family. The son had prospered, and little wonder seeing he was the eyes and ears of the factor in the place. That was Seamus Sionnach, the ground officer.

If we had grievances it was to the ground officer we were supposed to make them known, and the ground officer had the authority to take our grievances to the factor. But no man in his right mind would have complained to Seamus Sionnach, for he was not to be trusted, seeing he had only one end in view—his own advancement.

Many a one knew that to their cost. A complaint to Seamus Sionnach and that was you branded as a trouble-maker in the eyes of the factor. Before long eviction would come, and you would see your land being worked by a brother or a cousin or a nephew of the ground officer—and he was not lacking in blood relations, the same one.

That is the worst of it when a factor has no Gaelic. The tongue of the people is in another man's mouth, as the saying has it, for the people never know what the ground officer is telling the factor about them.

You may wonder how such a rag of a man got the job of ground officer in the first place. Well, they say it was because of the great things he did as a young man in the war. That was long ago, but he still boasted that his head had been almost cleft in two by the sabre of a Russian dragoon, and right enough he had a fearsome scar on the top of his head. You never saw him without a bonnet outside the kirk. But there were some who made out he had got the blow nearer home, that it was the work of a fisherman in Stornoway who had caught the bold lad with a hand in his purse. Whatever the truth of the matter, it was plain that the blow had not affected his wits. If ever a man earned his nickname, it was Seamus Sionnach, for he was truly as fly as a fox.

He led the clapping as the *Maighstir* got to his feet, and there were few who did not bring their hands together when they saw his quick eyes on them.

All the *Maighstir* had to do was introduce the factor, and you would have thought that was a quick job seeing every man in the place knew fine who he was. But no, he had to go on for long enough, that caught up in his speech making out he never saw the daggers of looks the factor was giving him. And I swear he made those who thought they knew English afraid to open their mouths in that tongue seeing he was laying off his chest in great long words as foreign to them as those of a heathen savage.

But I will say this for the factor: he did not take half so long. He did not have to. If you are declaring war, there is no need to wrap it up in fancy words.

There was to be a rent collection on 1st November. The lairds could not pay their share of rates and taxes unless they got their rents. Those who had arrears of rent (and that was everyone in the place) must clear them on 1st November, or pay as much as they were able. If they failed to make payment, their goods and cattle would be seized, and they would be evicted from the land.

When the factor sat down, it was the turn of Seamus Sionnach to rise and put his master's words into the Gaelic, for the most of them there were not versed in English. But the fly fellow had his own way of shaping the factor's message.

"Friends, the laird is dead," he began, "and who would not grieve at the passing of so fine a man? Ach, many a one has said to me, a diamond of a man just, the laird, a very diamond of a man. And so he was. He had great schemes for this place, great schemes. But he was not spared to carry them out, and now he is gone, and his daughter is without a father, and the lawyers in Edinburgh are creating something terrible because the estate has to pay big taxes. And where is the money to come from when you are all holding back rents that are the due o' the laird's daughter?

"Times are bad, right enough. I know, I know. Prices are poor, right enough. Amn't I the one who knows?—me who lost heavy at the sales. But our fathers knew bad times; many a bad winter they faced in their day. There was the year o' the great famine in '46 when the crops failed and folk were that far gone in hunger they had to bleed their beasts for food. But still an' all they managed to put enough by for the rent. They were honest men, our fathers, honest men—men to be proud of.

"There are some who say the Government will pay the arrears. Fine I know them. Fine I know Lachlann Ban was one wi' that lie on his lips. But where is the bold fellow to-day? Waiting for the Government to pay his rent? Not him. The same one has cleared out o' the place and is making for America. You think he will be sending over your rent in American dollars? Not him.

"Lachlann Ban was after making lies, deceiving you just. The factor has been to London, speaking to big men in the Government, and this is the word he brings: The Government say the rents must be paid, or there will be trouble—terrible trouble.

"Right enough, what else can we expect? If we fail to pay our rents the lairds cannot pay their taxes, and if the lairds cannot pay their taxes we are done for, friends. That will be an end to a proper schooling for our children. There will be no more roads for us. Aye, and what of the paupers?

I am telling you, the paupers will be roaming the country like wolves when there is not so much as a dry crust provided for them.

"Make no mistake, it is the poor will suffer the most if authority is not obeyed. Is there anyone here wants to see poor widow women turned from their homes—and for why? Because you have among you men who will not take the honest way and pay what is owing. Close your ears to their lies. If you listen to them they will bring ruin on the place.

"Friends, there is to be a rent collection on 1st November. I ask every one o' you to make payment on that day. If you fail, as sure as fate, the Government will send the marines in to uphold the law. If the rent is not paid, it is ruin for you, black ruin. Cattle poinded, fodder seized—aye, and every bit o' gear to be found in a house. Every bit, mind. Meal chests, bed, bedding, tables, chairs, spinning-wheels— everything you can put a name to.

"So listen to me, friends, and take the honest course. Pay the rents you are owing so we can keep our schools open and get more roads and save the paupers from starvation and keep up the good name o' the place and prosper together the way our fathers before us did. And give to that poor bairn, the laird's daughter, her just due."

They clapped him! As sure as I am here, they clapped him! Clapped Seamus Sionnach, the biggest rogue in creation! Not all of them, mind. But enough. More than enough, by my way of it. Some of them near the front started to cheer, clowns that they were. Well, I am telling you, it is wonderful the way people can be bewitched by words. The man had put a spell on them.

And he was in his glory, the same one, bowing and waving, that false smile of his fairly splitting his face from ear to ear. The clapping and the cheering were meat and drink to him. I do not believe a full jug of whisky—and he liked his whisky, Seamus Sionnach—could have put him in better form.

Until the shouts came from outside. The smile was gone from his face as swift as if he had dipped his hand into a full purse and found it empty. But I did not need to hear the name they were crying. I had eyes. From my stance in the lobby, I could see twin sheets of flame rising high in the night sky across the river. They cast a crimson glow about a white house, the only house in our township—apart from the manse and the schoolhouse—with a slated roof. It was the house of Seamus Sionnach. And the flames rose from his burning stackyard and peat stack.

3

I was out of the lobby and racing across the yard before the headlong rush from the school started. I stopped at the school gates, eyes fixed on the great gouts of flame rising high across the river straight in front of me, undecided whether to take the road round by the bridge or make straight down to the river and chance the short-cut by the stepping stones. But before I could move hands seized my arm in a grip that was not to be denied, and I was dragged into the narrow gap between the wall and the side of the factor's coach, out of the path of the crowd making for the gates.

It was the *cailleach*. We stood in a yellow pool of light cast by the coach lamps, and I could see she was dressed in her best Sabbath coat and bonnet, she who never ventured beyond the narrow circle of hearth and byre except to go to the kirk or a prayer meeting. And there was no prayer meeting on to-night with every single man in the place—save those too burdened with a weight of years and infirmity to rise from their beds—assembled to meet the factor. I wondered what the *cailleach* was doing down at the school at a meeting of men when even the mother of Lachlann Ban—she who had once felled four policemen with a swing of her great iron cooking pot—did not show face. But such thoughts were not with me for long. I was too eager to be off, and I got angry at the way she continued to cling to my arm, as if she had not clapped eyes on me for years and could not bear to let me out of her sight again. But when I tried to shake myself free, she tightened her grip.

"Let me away," I muttered, aware of the coachman screwing his head round, curious to know what we were about. "I am off to see the fire."

The rest of them would be over the bridge by now and hastening up the path to Seamus Sionnach's croft. Even Old Diarmad, who was turned eighty and bad on his legs, would be there before me.

"Not you," she cried, her voice shrill—and it was unlike her to be heedless of the cocked ears of a stranger. "You are coming with me to see the *Maighstir*, boy."

"The *Maighstir*?"

"Aye, he has something to tell you—and mind you thank him the first chance you get. It is not everyone in the *Maighstir's* position would take the trouble, I am telling you. So mind your manners, boy, or it is me you will have to reckon with."

"Trouble?" I said, in a right daze by now, and not getting her meaning at all. "What trouble?"

"Wait you," she said, tugging me along the path to the schoolhouse. "You will hear soon enough from Himself. I promised I would not say a word, and neither I will."

"Ach, the *Maighstir* can wait," I said. "Let go of my arm. I am off wi' the rest to see the fire."

Now that we were out of the circle of light cast by the lamps of the coach, she stopped and shook me. And she was not lacking in strength, the *cailleach*, for all her slight frame. Those arms of hers had lifted creels of sea-ware from the shore and carried them up the steeply winding path through the break in the cliffs to the croft; had sowed and harrowed and garnered the crops, and done all the work of the croft for which our father was not able. I am telling you, she shook me as if I had been a boy of seven, not a grown man of seventeen.

"Are you wise, boy?" she flared, fairly stammering the words out she was that wild. "Many a one would go down on their knees before the *Maighstir* for the half of what he has done for you. Now, no more o' your nonsense, or I will be after dying of shame before we get the length o' the schoolhouse door."

Miss Nicolson, the *Maighstir's* sister, was waiting at the open back door, her small mouth pursed in a tight smile. I wondered how long she had been standing there, and if she had heard the *cailleach* laying off her chest at me.

"Come away in," she murmured, poking her neck out like a hen reaching for thinly scattered grain, and speaking in a breathless whisper, the way she always did, as if there were hidden listeners all around, desperate keen to know what she was saying.

The *cailleach* perched on the edge of a straight-backed chair in the far corner of the room. When I settled down in the big, comfortable chair by the fire, she had to cry, "What are you thinking of, boy? That is the *Maighstir's* chair."

And Miss Nicolson had to fuss me, as I knew she would, and pat my shoulder, and say, "No, no, sit, sit, Alasdair. Duncan is still with the major, and, ah, when they come in they, ah, will be going into the front room."

Another pat on my shoulder, and then she was off fussing about the room, straightening cloths on the backs of the chairs, taking a brush to the spotless, gleaming hearth, flicking here and there at what I suppose she imagined to be specks of dust, and for ever darting to the window and peering round the drawn blinds to see if she could spy the coming of the factor and her brother. And all the time the *cailleach* sat perched bolt upright on the edge of her chair, mouth buttoned tight shut, hands folded quiet in her lap, giving me daggers of looks every time Miss Nicolson's back was turned.

When the front door creaked open, the *Maighstir's* sister was off like a startled hare. The *cailleach* beckoned urgently to me. "They will be taking the factor into the front room," she whispered. "When you are called in, speak only when you are spoken to, mind, and be sure to sir them every time."

Before I could ask her what was on the go, the *Maighstir* entered with his sister fussing along at his elbow. The *cailleach* was on her feet in an instant, her eyes shouting at me to rise.

"Sit down, sit down," said the *Maighstir*, moving across and straddling the hearth rug, as if he was about to take up his stance before the blackboard, his big bony hands and wrists looking as naked as a fresh peeled onion the awkward way they stuck out from his cuffs.

"Major Traill is riding post-haste to Uig," he announced. "I fear he is determined to telegraph Sheriff Ivory in Inverness to seek aid in, ah, a proper enforcement of the law. I must say that was an, ah, dastardly deed to-night, the firing of the ground officer's peat stack and all his winter feed." He looked sternly at me, although I had not said a word. "No good can come from such lawless acts, boy."

"Well, they cannot put the blame on us," I said. "Every man in the place was at the meeting to-night."

"True, true," the *Maighstir* agreed, stroking his chin and tipping his head back to gaze up at his fine plaster ceiling, a sure sign that he was not agreeing at all and would be back to deal with me as soon as he had put his thoughts in order, "all the men were at the meeting. But is it equally true that, ah, only a man is, ah, capable of applying a burning brand to a stackyard? I take it, Alasdair, you would have us believe"—here he paused, and enfolded his sister and the *cailleach* with a knowing smile, the two of them fine pleased to respond in kind, although they were no wiser than me when it came to the bit—"that, ah, none but the male sex would know how to kindle a peat stack into flame?"

"How do you mean?" I said.

"I would suggest, Alasdair, that the work of destruction" —another pause, while he pinched his chin between his long middle fingers and fixed his owlish stare on me, well aware that he would never want for an approving audience so long as his sister and the *cailleach* were about—" could have been, ah, adequately carried out by one of the, ah, weaker sex."

"A woman!" I exclaimed. "Ach, never the day. No woman would have the nerve."

The *Maighstir* hoisted into position the thin smile he always wore when he was certain sure he was in the right. "You have a short memory, boy," he said. "Three years ago—last 17th April, to be precise—Sheriff Ivory marched on the township of Braes with fifty Glasgow policemen under his command. There was a battle, as you very well know, and the sheriff's force was compelled to retire in some, ah, disorder. Think carefully now when I tell you the names of the people of Braes who were injured in that battle." He ticked them off on his fingers, one by one. "Ann Nicolson, Kate Finlayson, Flora Nicolson, Marion Nicolson, Kate MacInnes and Mary Nicolson. All members of the, ah, weaker sex, but all prepared to stand like Amazons and do battle with the police."

"Ach, they were a disgrace to the place," the *cailleach* cried, unable to contain herself.

"Be quiet," I said, fairly spitting the words at her, too disgusted to care what she thought, the shame strong in me that she should have remained standing all this time, although the *Maighstir* himself had told her to sit.

It would have been war there and then, if Miss Nicolson had not babbled, "I declare, I do declare, it is true what they say about a watched kettle. But there it is, boiling at last. Now we will soon have the tea on the go." And she hurried to the fire: "You had best tell Alasdair what the factor had to say, Duncan."

"Ah, yes, yes," he said. "Indeed, yes." He gave his nervous squawk of a laugh. "I confess in the excitement of the, ah, events of the evening, I quite forgot."

"But you were not after forgetting to speak to the factor," said the *cailleach*, that humble you would have thought she was addressing a prince of the blood royal. "That was terrible good of you, Mr. Nicolson, and I know fine Alasdair is heart grateful to you, heart grateful just." Her eyes dared me to say her nay. But I was not for saying a word until I knew what was on the go.

"I had intended to take Major Traill back to the house after the meeting to discuss Alasdair's future with him," he went on, tipping his head back and speaking to the ceiling, "but that, ah, was not to be. However, I did mention to him the laird's, ah, elaborate plans for the boy, and I think he is, ah, not unmindful of the,˙ ah, obligation to be discharged."

The face of the *cailleach* was a study. She thought she was a great hand at the English, but in truth she was lost once the *Maighstir* got going on his humming and hawing, no more aware than a dancing dervish of the meaning of the great monsters of words he was so fond of rolling off his tongue. She was not understanding him at all, not until he suddenly stopped studying the ceiling, clapped me on the back, and brayed, "You are to take the mail coach to Uig in the morning, boy. The factor will be waiting to see you in his office."

She understood that all right, and she sat down for the first time since the *Maighstir* had entered the room. Not from any lack of respect, you understand, but because she had to. I knew her well enough to realise that the strength had gone from her legs, and it was easy to see why. She had done great things by her way of it, and herself a humble woman not given to questioning the actions of her superiors. She was the one who had got the *Maighstir* to speak to Major Traill, and it was because of her work that the factor had summoned me to Uig. And her mind ran free from there. Uig was the first step on the road to Edinburgh and a right schooling to lift me clear of the toil of the croft and place me within the rare circle of those who enjoyed the favour of the gentry. We might be under threat of eviction, and the lash of Sheriff Ivory's law, but the *cailleach* was not worrying so long as the factor was pleased to smile upon me.

She said as much, when at last we got clear of the schoolhouse, fairly savouring the words, as if each one was a choice morsel to be tasted slowly, "Well, boy, it is a blessing just that I got the *Maighstir* to speak to the factor. I believe it was God's will that the major should have been in the place to-night."

"To tell us we would be forced from our homes if the rent is not paid?"

"Ach, the rent!" She gave a sniff that said more than words. "The rent is the laird's just due and must be paid and that is all there is about it. In my father's day the rent was set aside once a beast was sold, and never touched supposing there was not a bite o' food in the house. In my father's day folk would ha' died rather than not pay the laird his rent. But it is changed days now, I am telling you, folk without a scrap o' pride expecting everything for nothing, and idle wastrels that busy making trouble wi' their tongues they have no thought o' work. You are well out of it, boy, and the sooner the better. Now that the factor wants to see you in Uig, that is you——"

"On your way to Edinburgh," I finished for her.

"Aye, for sure," she said, too uplifted with dreams of glory to perceive I was mocking her. "The factor is not the man to take you all the way to Uig supposing he was not for carrying out the wishes o' the laird. You will need to be up at the crack, mind, and have all your gear packed ready for off. It would be terrible altogether if you missed the mail coach, and the factor waiting on you. We must make certain sure——" She broke off, suddenly aware that I had moved away from her. "Wait, boy." She snatched at my arm, but I was too quick for her. "Where are you away to, Alasdair? The fire is out long since. Come back. You are needing an early bed, boy. If you miss——" Her voice grew thin and was swept away in the sough of the wind, lost entire in the empty dark of the night as I ran for the river and the stepping stones.

There was a good flow of water in the river, the stones awash and greasy. But I made the crossing safely enough, taking my time, measuring the distance and leaping carefully from stone to stone. I was poised on the last stone, ready to spring to the far bank, when something moved in the darkness ahead of me. I shifted my footing, and very near plunged into the river. Recovering my balance, I crouched forward, listening. Right enough, there was something moving, a blacker shape against the night sky.

And then my nostrils curled as I sniffed the sickly, over-powering, unmistakable stench of a billy goat in rut.

The beast belonged to Ailean Mor, an old man who stayed by himself in a ruin of a house close by the river with only the black billy for company. All the *bodachs* said he had been a great scholar in his day, able to read and write English and himself never inside a school, but he was blind of an eye now and not right in the head, taking many a queer turn when the moon was full, walking by the river in the dead of night, singing psalms and calling on sinners to repent. There were some who said he had foretold the coming of the great flood that had swept the laird's lodge into the sea, and there was not a man in the place who did not believe he had the gift of the second sight.

I can tell you I did not much fancy meeting the like of Ailean Mor by the river on a dark night, and in truth I fancied facing his black goat even less. The beast was pawing the ground, and making queer, strangled moaning cries deep in his chest as he worked himself into a fury. I knew fine the moment I set foot on land he would lower his evil, horned head and charge.

"Away!" I cried, wishing I could turn on the slippery stone and make back the way I had come. "Away you go!" And whistled shrilly—clown that I was—to try to make the beast believe I had a dog within call. That was a poor hope. There was not a dog in the place with the heart to tackle the black goat, and fine the brute knew it. He came on down the bank, panting and snorting like the Devil himself, the terrible stench off him fairly turning my stomach.

"Well, well, it is yourself, Alasdair," a soft voice said. "You are late on the go, boy."

He had a silent step on him, Ailean Mor, and the same one

could see better in the dark with his one eye than I could with two.

I leapt to the bank, taking care to keep Ailean Mor between me and the goat. But he spoke to the beast as if it had been a Christian in trousers, and as sure as I am here it wandered off quietly.

"I was for taking a look at the fire," I said, still getting a terrible stench of goat, for all that the beast had moved away. Ailean Mor was that well acquaint with the smell it did not put him up or down.

"The fire?" he said. "Too late, boy. Ashes, all ashes. That is the way of it in this world, fire to ashes, cold and dead."

The waning moon slipped clear of the clouds, and I got a glimpse of his face, lined and seamed and black as an old piece of dried out peat, his sightless eye a pucker of wrinkled skin, the beard on him as thin and straggling as that of his goat. A scud of clouds covered the pale moon, and the wind struck chill as it gusted down from the hill.

"Well, if there is nothing to see, I had best away home," I said.

"They came from the sea," Ailean Mor said, his soft, dreamy voice near drowned in the noisy rush of the river, "and the stranger went away by the sea. Him wi' the beard as gold as corn, and a ring o' bright gold in his ear." He gripped my shoulder, and put his face close to mine, the stench of rutting goat off him something terrible. "I saw the coming o' the stranger wi' the bright ring o' gold in his ear, saw him breathing fire the night the moon was full."

His good eye gazed beyond me down river, as if he perceived some new vision in the dark of night, but his sightless eye—that puckered hollow of parchment like skin—seemed to be searching my face. I felt his grip tightening on my shoulder. "Do you believe me, boy?" he whispered.

"Aye," I said, swallowing hard all of a sudden. "I believe you."

Ailean Mor let go of my shoulder. We stood facing each other for perhaps as long as it takes to draw breath, and then I was away, leaping from stone to stone as if my feet had taken wing. When I reached the bank, I did not stop to look back.

4

The long white house of the factor was as big as a kirk, and it might well have been one, if the respectful silence of those gathered outside was anything to go by. In our township, the Uig folk had always had the name of being terrible stiff with strangers, and right enough not one of them waiting there had a word for me. They were that subdued the *Maighstir* would have been fine pleased to have had them in his class at the school.

The house stood above the road looking down on the walled park of the laird's ruined lodge and taking in the full sweep of the landlocked bay. The rising ground behind the house had been made into a terraced garden, the steep banks of the terraces clothed in trees and shrubs. The garden was that big a man and a boy laboured constantly to keep it in trim, but seen against the towering face of the hill it was no more than the clipped nail on the toe of a giant. The hill reared high, shielding the bay from the east, its green face cleft by hungry streams greedy to reach the sea, and scarred an ugly black where the great flood had brought down landslips, stripping the rock bare.

The *Maighstir* had said the factor would be waiting for me. That was a lie for a start. It was me who had to do the waiting, feeling a right clown as I hung about the fringe of the silent crowd at the gate. From time to time the green door of the house was opened by a grey, stooped *bodach*, gold-rimmed spectacles on his long nose, who would summon

44

one of them by name. Each time the man so called would snatch the bonnet from his head and hasten inside, that swift to answer the call you would think there were riches in store for him.

The man at the door seemed to know them all well enough, and as often as not was all smiles when he let them out again. But when I plucked up courage to speak to him —and eleven men, and a *cailleach* with a boy younger than me along with her, had been admitted by then—there was no trace of a smile upon his face. He peered down at me over the top of his spectacles, for all the world as if I was some freak the like of which he had never encountered before. "Bide your time, boy," he snapped, "the factor has business enough to deal with before he can attend to the like o' you," and it was then that I saw him for what he was, a grey withered husk of a man, that proud to be keeping the door for the factor he was in his glory if he could turn a body back.

As the day wore on, and the pale October sun dropped behind the shoulder of the headland, blackening the circling hills, I was certain sure they had forgotten me. Or worse, that the factor had never had any intention of seeing me, that he had been having the *Maighstir* on, and the same one too soft in the head to see it. Good grief, I would look a right idiot trailing all the way home to report that I had not so much as clapped eyes on the factor, let alone spoken to him. The *cailleach* would never believe me. She was that taken up in her dreams of glory she would be picturing me driven to Edinburgh in the factor's own coach. Well, if not to Edinburgh, at least the length of Portree, so that I could board the *Clydesdale* in style. Indeed, it would be easier to convince her that I had seen the ghost of her father, the old *Ceistear*, leading a drunken revel in the burial ground of a Sabbath night than get her to believe that this was the factor's idea of a joke.

Of all the crowd who had been waiting to gain an audience of the factor I was the only one left. I was on the point of making off when the green door opened—and this time it opened for me. The man with the gold spectacles beckoned impatiently, as if it was himself who had been waiting for hours unnoticed, and I found myself standing before Major Traill, unable—if the truth be told—to repress a shiver, for all the roarer of a fire that blazed in the room.

The factor was busy writing. He did not pause in his work to glance up, or even so much as raise his eyes. I began to wonder if he had heard the door open and knew that I was standing before him. But I was not so foolish as to speak before I was spoken to, which was as well for me.

"Stewart," he said, at length, breaking a silence that had endured for so long the sound of my own breathing had become terrible harsh in my ears. "Alexander Stewart, is it not?"

"Yes, sir," I said.

His cold blue eyes lifted slowly from his desk, fastened on my face and travelled slowly down to my feet. I was wearing a split new suit made from a length of good tweed gifted to the *cailleach* by her brother, a weaver in Portnalong. She had done the tailoring herself, and as she had made the suit to allow for growth my hands were lost in the sleeves of the coat. I put them behind my back, away from the cold, blue eyes of the factor.

"What makes you think the estate should find work for you?" he said suddenly.

When I made no move to speak—and in truth I did not know what to say—he rapped, "Well? Answer, boy."

"It is not for the estate to find me work," I stammered.

"No? Mr. Nicolson seemed to be of the opinion that you entertained great expectations."

"No, sir," I said. "Not since the laird died."

"Ah!" He sounded fine pleased all of a sudden; why, I knew not. "You think General Kemball-Denison would have installed you in this office? Trained you to be factor, perhaps?"

"No, sir," I said, knowing fine he was mocking me, and busy storing his words in my mind for use against the *cailleach*. It was her work that had landed me before him, defenceless, unable to escape the lash of his tongue.

"So you were not expecting to find work here?"

"No, sir, not since the laird died."

"But if the General was still with us, what then?"

"I don't know, sir."

"When did you leave school?"

"Three years—no, four years ago, sir."

"How old were you when you left?"

"Thirteen, sir."

"Thirteen, eh?" The way he said it you would think I had done murder. He fingered his smooth shaven chin. "And you think you have the education to fit you for work in the estate office?"

"No, sir, that is why Mr. Nicolson was after giving me lessons, and . . . "

"And what?" he demanded, eager as a ferret getting the scent of blood.

"The laird spoke to me," I mumbled, "about a school in Edinburgh."

"Did he, indeed?" he said softly, eyebrows arching in mock surprise. He moistened his lips with his tongue, and he might well have been honing a blade for when he spoke again his voice had a cutting edge that bit deep. "The laird is dead, boy, and you can take it from me that the estate is in no position to finance your further education. Do you understand?"

"Yes, sir."

"A few years in a village school is no preparation for work that requires some education. Is that understood?"

"Yes, sir."

"But we may be able to find you something in keeping with your abilities, if you are prepared to apply yourself to your duties and give your master no cause for complaint." He handed me an envelope, sealed in wax. "Take this to Mr. Gordon at the inn. It is a letter from me. If I know Mr. Gordon, he will do his best for you."

The factor was not the only one who knew Mr. Gordon. Indeed, the innkeeper was known to every man in the place, and not by the stiff English Mister the factor used. In the Gaelic, he was Uilleam Mor, and Uilleam Mor was not only the innkeeper, he was the tacksman of Glenuig as well, with more cattle and sheep to his name than the whole of our township put together, and the same one desperate keen to add to his stock. When my father was young Glenuig was worked by crofters, but they had been driven from their land to the shore, and that was how Uilleam Mor came by his tack.

The *bodach* named him for a pure rogue, but there were plenty in the place with a good word for him, and that should not surprise you when you know more about the man. Uilleam Mor spoke the Gaelic, and spoke it well, as if he had learned it at his mother's knee. There were not many tacksmen who did, the most of them being incomers, despising the old language as fit only for savages, although the English they were so proud of sounded coarse enough to my ears. But it was more than just the language; it was the way he treated people. Uilleam Mor did not hold to the English ways. He never passed any man by—not even supposing he was a pauper, living on the charity of the parish —without giving him a cheery greeting in his own tongue, although you would have thought they would have had the wits to see that only a fool would neglect to get folk in a good mood before doing business with them. And if you had a beast for sale—and who had not?—the chances were you would be doing business with Uilleam Mor, sooner or later.

Mind you, I was well pleased to have him laying off at me in the Gaelic after the cold, stiff, withdrawn English of the factor.

"Well, well, boy, come away in," he cried, as I hung back behind the fair-haired maid who had guided me to his room; a cosy, cluttered cupboard of a room, not like the factor's orderly office where even the scuttle for coals (the factor did not cut peats; he had coals shipped by barque from Glasgow) had a polish you could see your face in. "What brings you this length from home, Alasdair?" His huge hand swallowed the envelope I held out, and he did not so much as glance at it. "Alasdair *mhic* Alasdair Rob it is, amn't I right?" he said.

Alasdair was my father's name as well as my own, and Rob the name of his father. That is the way men are spoken of in this place.

"Aye, I knew fine," he went on when I nodded, repeating again, "Alasdair the son of Alasdair Rob. Ach, there is not a face in this place I am not for putting a name on. Fine I know your father, boy. Many's the beast I bought from him. Aye, and paid dear for them, too, let me tell you. A man with an eye for a good cattle beast, your father, and the same one not easy beaten down from his price. Many's the time he squeezed me for more than I was for paying, and you know what he would do when we had clasped hands on the deal? Miscall me for doing him down! Give me dogs' abuse just!"

Uilleam Mor laughed until his great belly shook and his small eyes slitted up into rolls of fat. The girth on him was something terrible. His tailor must have been a good hand for the cloth of his trouser was taking fearful punishment with that monster of a belly straining against it.

He went on for long enough, speaking of this one and that in our township, wanting to know how it was with them, what like a harvest they had garnered, were their beasts in good trim, and such like, the questions coming thick and fast, and all the time the factor's letter—and it sealed in wax—crushed in his great fist as if it was of no more account than a note from a beggar.

But he came to it in his own good time, holding the letter at arm's length and nodding to himself as he read. He stuffed it into his pocket, and looked at me for a long moment before he spoke, his small, sharp eyes searching my face, as if he saw something new in me all of a sudden, and was at a loss to know why.

"Well, well," he said, "you must rank high wi' the factor, boy. He is keen on me giving you a start at the Inn, and Major Traill is not the man to advance a person unless he is certain sure they are worth their salt. Well, what do you say, boy? Am I to take heed o' your high and mighty friends and take you on, eh?" He gave one of his deep, rumbling laughs, setting his jowls aquiver and his belly shaking. "A poor man like me must take heed o' the factor, that is the way of it, eh? Well, Alasdair, I will tell you straight, I think you and me will get along fine, and I believe I have the very job for you. Mind you, I would have a queue stretching the length of Idrigill supposing folk here knew I was needing a stableboy. You are in luck, boy. And it is a job that will suit you fine. A grand bothy in the loft above the stables, fine and snug and the place all to yourself. Three good meals a day and a jug o' best porter along wi' your supper. At night you lend a hand in the taproom. Plenty work, boy, make no mistake about that, but it is myself will see you right at the end o' the day if you put your back into it and work with a will. Well, what do you say?"

I nodded dumbly, and he went rattling on, "I have a wagon load o' fodder going over your way to-morrow. The driver can call and tell your folk you are settled in fine and snug at the inn, and bring back any working gear you are needing." He reached out and fingered the sleeve of my coat. "That is a grand piece o' tweed, but the *bodach* will not be pleased supposing you are for working in the stables with his good suit on your back."

I saw his great belly starting to shake, and I could feel my cheeks flaming. "The suit is not my father's," I cried. "It was made special for me from a new length o' tweed I had from my uncle in Portnalong."

Uilleam Mor's laugh choked in his throat, but his voice was as cheery as ever when he said, "Well, then, you will just need to be putting on some beef to fill it out," and I wondered if I had been mistaken in imagining a sudden flash of anger in his eyes. He heaved himself up out of his chair, and went to the door. "Iain!" he roared. "Iain!"

A thin, dark young fellow came running, knowing eyes making a quick search of my face the moment he was inside the door. "Iain, we have got a new stableboy," Uilleam Mor said. "Young Alasdair here,"—He gave my shoulder a friendly squeeze, and I swear the bone very near cracked—

"and himself near perishing o' hunger I would not wonder. Away to the kitchen with him, and see he gets a good bite o' supper. And after you have shown him the stables, get him to give you a hand in the taproom. Off with you now, or Alasdair will be thinking there is never a stroke o' work done in this place." His rumbling laugh chased us all the way to the kitchen, and he could well afford to laugh seeing he knew fine that the pair of us would be on the go until long after midnight.

There was a huge range in the stone-flagged kitchen, roaring as fierce as the forge in Colla's smithy back home, the old wife busy at the cooking near roasting, her face a mottled crimson. But she was not too busy to see that I got a topper of a feed, she and the fair-haired maid, whose name was the same as my mother's, Murdina.

I had a big bowl of broth, potatoes galore, and more butcher meat than our whole family would have seen in a twelvemonth. And if that was not enough for any man, Murdina placed a heaped bowl of semolina and cream before me. Mind you, I would have enjoyed the feed even more if only the dark fellow had left me in peace. From the moment he sat down beside me his tongue was never idle, and from the way he spoke you would have thought Uig another Glasgow, the inn the favourite calling place of all the gentry in Scotland, and himself their close familiar. But once he discovered where I came from his whole manner changed, and I might well have fancied myself one of the gentry seeing the respectful way he addressed me.

His sharp eyes scoured the kitchen, made sure the cook was busy with her pots and pans at the range, and Murdina, bent over the sink, had her back to us, before he said softly, "You fairly sorted that rogue of a ground officer in your township. The news is all over the place, how his peat stack and every bite of his winter feed—six big stacks of hay, they say, and four o' corn—went up in flames, and Himself laying off his chest in front o' the factor at the time." He poked me in the ribs, making me spill a spoonful of semolina. "That took some nerve, I am telling you."

"Aye, it took some nerve," I said.

"They are saying it was the women, but I——"

"Women?" I spluttered, near choking on a mouthful of pudding. "Never the day! What woman would have the nerve to fire a stackyard?"

"Right enough," he said eagerly, drawing his chair closer to mine. He brushed a lock of black hair out of his eyes, and inspected the kitchen, all in the one quick movement. The same one would never be taken unawares, that was a sure thing. "Right enough," he repeated, "that is just——"

A bell jangled at our back. "Taproom, Iain," Murdina called.

As the dark fellow pushed back his chair and hurried out, she picked up my empty bowl, and wiped the table clean. Her fair hair brushed my face. "Watch what you say to Iain Dubh," she whispered. "That fellow is the ears of Uilleam Mor."

She was gone before I could speak, and was no sooner bent over the sink than the dark fellow was back at my elbow. "We had best get moving," he said. "They are starting coming in, and once there is a crowd in the taproom that is me on the go steady."

He took me out to the stables at the back of the inn, past three great monsters of peat stacks, the biggest I had ever seen.

"That lot would make a rare blaze, eh?" he said, seeing my eyes on them.

I nodded, thinking of the labour that had gone into the

winning of them; the toil to strip the tough turf, the back-breaking work of the cutting and spreading, the patient lifting of them—once the sun and air had hardened the top side—into tiny pyramids to dry, and the long haul with the dried peats from the bog to the inn. "Well, I wouldn't fancy cutting that load," I said. "You must have been hard at it for weeks just."

"Not me," he said, disdainful as a lord. "It is easy done, if you know how. See you, every man in this place is after owing money to Uilleam Mor. If they are not owing him for fodder, or a barrel or two o' salt herring, or oil for their lamps, they are in debt to him for drink. Once a fine spell o' weather comes along in the spring, Uilleam Mor marches into the taproom and says, 'I could be doing wi' a hand at the peats, boys,' and they come running. Aye, by the score just. It is easy seen why he has the biggest peat stacks you ever clapped eyes on."

He led the way up the ladder to the loft. It was dark in the loft, the sweet smell of hay all around, the only sound the quiet breath of the horses in their stalls below. It was a warm, cosy, secretive dark, friendly as a familiar blanket drawn tight around you in your own bed at night.

"Where are you?" Iain Dubh said.

"Here."

The boards creaked as he moved towards me. I felt his breath on my face. He must have been drinking porter, for the smell of beer was strong in my nostrils. He gripped my arm. "I believe it was yourself put the torch to the ground officer's stacks," he whispered.

"Not me," I said, pleased enough that he should credit me with the nerve for such a deed.

"Who then?"

"Who?" I repeated foolishly, not wanting to rid him of

the notion that I was the fire-raiser, and unwilling to let on that I was no wiser than himself.

"Aye, who then?" he said.

"How should I know?" I countered.

"Ach, you know fine." He sighed in vexation, and withdrew his hand from my arm. "Good grief, if it was me that knew I would be right proud to say the name. That fellow, the ground officer—that Seamus Sionnach—is a right rag of a man. Many's the one I heard call him that, and worse." He gripped my arm again. "You know what I think? He should have been put off the cliff, the same one, long ago."

"*Dhia*," I said, "that would be murder."

Green eyes gleamed at me unblinking in the darkness. The cat streaked past my feet and vanished. I hoped Iain Dubh had not noticed the start I gave.

"Murder?" he said, and laughed. "Was it not murder when the same one spoke lies to the factor and had old folk cleared from their crofts and hastened to the grave? Was that not murder?"

"Maybe so." I hesitated, torn between revealing that I was as ignorant as himself and letting him persist in the belief that I was important enough not only to know about everything that went on in our township, but to have a hand in the doing of it.

A roar from without, loud enough to have stirred the dead in the new burial ground high on the hill above the inn, saved me from making up my mind. It was Uilleam Mor summoning the dark fellow. Iain Dubh was not slow in cursing his master, but he lost no time in finding his way to the ladder, and was back inside the inn before I emerged from the stables.

I will say this for him, though, he was a worker. Mind you, he had to be. The taproom was crowded, men crammed tight, shoulder to shoulder, on the wooden benches around the walls, and others on their feet in a solid wedge from the counter to the far wall, all of them it seemed clamouring for drink at the same time.

The low-ceilinged room was thick with tobacco smoke, lying heavy in wreathed coils and the deafening clatter grew louder as the night progressed, such a babel of tongues at work that words grew swollen and misshapen, coming together like the clashing of giant cymbals, and merging into a great trumpet blast of sound. The noise beat about my ears, and as sure as I am here I was made stupid by the din, not catching Iain Dubh's shouted commands at all, and rushing hither and thither with drinks, vainly trying to follow his pointing finger, for all the world like a deaf mute at a fair.

It was a relief to me when I had to haul in peats for the fires, and I am telling you there were some fires on the go in that place. The big kitchen range alone devoured peats that fast it was little wonder Uilleam Mor needed all the menfolk in the village to secure his supply for him.

At every fill of the creel, I rested against the peat stack, bathing my sweating face in the cool night air, and looking down at the lights of the fishing smacks, riding at anchor in the still pool of the bay below. The inn was perched half-way up the hill beyond the Conon river, and the fishermen must have seen it as a bright beacon of light against the dark of the towering headland. It was queer to think of men down there maybe staring up at the lighted inn, and hankering after the noise and the company, wanting away from their boats where there was only the quiet wash of the tide to contend with their talk.

There was no more resting for me once Uilleam Mor called for fuel. I was on the trot up and down the narrow stairs to the parlour, where he entertained his special cronies, until I had filled the huge wicker basket he kept for peats. That done, he led the way down the stone steps to the cellar, a lantern held high in one hand, his ring of keys swinging on a leather thong in the other, happy as any careful jailer at the sight of the kegs of whisky and rum and the barrels of porter secure in the chill cavern of the cellar. He patted a keg of whisky, and said, "Make haste, boy, Iain is waiting on you."

I hefted the keg and hurried back to the taproom, and the heat and the sweat and the noise and the smoke. The blurred faces started to dance, and I had to grip the counter when I set down the keg. But if I felt bad then, by the time the last of them had gone—and I swear they would have been there yet but for Uilleam Mor jollying them to the door—I was fit to drop in my tracks and sleep where I fell.

Sleep? That was a good one. The taproom had to be swept out, the floor washed down, and glasses and mugs washed and stacked ready for the next day before I was free to take down a lantern from the kitchen and creep out, leaden-footed, to the loft above the stables.

I was passing the first of the peat stacks when I heard voices, speaking softly, not loud enough to make out the words, but voices sure enough. I stopped, and listened, and moved on again, treading lightly. The voices were louder, one of them a girl's. They came from behind the high stack, at the far end. I stopped again, undecided. Maybe it was Murdina, or one of the other maids, meeting her sweetheart on the sly.

A man's voice, deep and husky, said, "To-morrow. I will wait for an hour after the last one is away." His throaty chuckle sounded so close he could have been standing by my side. "After the fire, the flood. Before we are done not one o' them will rest easy o' nights."

A girl's voice answered him, too soft for me to catch the words. Not wanting to spy, but curious to know who was there, I tiptoed on to the end of the stack, the lantern held high.

They must have seen the light coming. Murdina met me at the end of the stack, blocking my view, but not before I had caught a glimpse of a bearded figure leaping for the shelter of the next peat stack.

"Why, Alasdair," she cried, shielding her eyes, "what a fright you gave me! I was after forgetting to shut the hens up. My word, Uilleam Mor would have been roaring in the morning supposing a fox had got in at them." A little nervous laugh bubbled from her lips, and she did it so well I was near believing her.

I lowered the lantern so that her face was in the shadows. "Who was the fellow with the beard?" I said.

"The fellow with the beard?" Her voice was a mocking echo. "You must have been dreaming, Alasdair." She laughed again. "Or seeing a ghost."

I watched her as she picked up her skirts and ran for the inn. If I had seen a ghost, I was in good company. So had Ailean Mor, and I was not blind of an eye like him. I had only caught a glimpse of the 'ghost', right enough, but I knew fine what I had seen. Indeed, I would swear on the Book to it.

His beard had been the colour of ripe corn, and even if I had been blind of an eye, like Ailean Mor, I could not have missed the ring of gold in his ear.

5

At home, the first one to be on the go in the morning was the *cailleach*. She would come through to the kitchen, where little Seoras and I shared the wall-bed, and fan the smouldering fire into fresh life, breaking dry peats across her knee, and fitting them into the crumbling, glowing embers, so that in no time at all the flames were leaping high, and there was hot tea waiting in the pot for us the moment we crawled out of bed. I never thought I would live to see the day when I would be hankering for the *cailleach* and her fussing, but I had to admit to myself that I could have done with her at the inn, first thing in the morning.

It seemed to me that I had no sooner laid down on the straw pallet in the loft, and drawn the blankets over my head, than I was being roughly shaken. The coachman was bent over me, a lantern gripped in his fist. His face was a leathery mask in the glare of the lamp; a fitting partner for the long, crooked shadow he cast across the steeply sloping roof.

"What ails you, boy?" he grumbled. "I was near taking the skin off my throat shouting up at you. I swear a dead man would ha' got up and danced, seeing the racket I was making, but you never stirred."

"What is it?" I mumbled, struggling into a sitting position, and trying to rub the sleep from my eyes.

"Time for up," he said, "and the coach made ready for

off, so be quick about it. You cannot keep the mails and the passengers waiting whatever."

That was a good one, seeing himself and his passengers would stop at every inn on the way back from Portree, and the worse the night the longer the stops, and the longer the stops the more the mails could go to pot for all they cared. Maybe it was the thought of the refreshments awaiting him at the inns on the road that made him so eager to be off. At any rate, he never stopped grumbling at me until the ponies were fed and watered, and harnessed between the shafts of the coach, and the mail baskets carried out from the inn and placed aboard. Even when he had climbed into his seat, and brought the reins down across the rumps of the two greys, he had to shout, "No more lying abed, mind, or I will be after taking a pail o' water to waken you."

Kirsty, the cook, said, "Ach, never take heed o' Sandy. He has a right scold of a wife, poor man, with a tongue on her that would sour good milk, so you cannot expect him to be in great form first thing when the wife has been on the go at him the long night through." She set down a big bowl of brose before me, the hot steam rising from the bowl that fragrant of nutty oatmeal I had to savour it with my nose before getting to work with a spoon. "But wait you, once the coach has climbed the brae, and the ponies are striding strong down to Glenhinesdale, Sandy will be singing away like a lintie—aye, even supposing it is bucketing down, and the day not fit for a tinker to take the road."

I could not imagine the coachman singing for joy, and I said as much. Old Kirsty stopped stirring the porridge pot long enough to give me a pitying look. "You have a lot to learn, boy," she said. "The older you get the thicker your shell—and, mind you, some folk build a queer prison of a shell for themselves. But there is always a key to them, supposing you have the patience to search for it."

It was not a key you would have needed for Davie Lindsay, but an axe, and one with a keen blade at that. Davie was Uilleam Mor's carrier, in charge of the big wagon that was used for carting heavy loads and delivering fodder and the like. He was a wee man from the east coast, the feet of him that small you would have taken him for a young boy if your first sight of him had been his boots. But he was no boy, not him; he was a man, well seasoned, as tough as tanned hide, a great worker, Davie, with not an idle bone in his body, and no taste at all for talk. Right enough, he was without the Gaelic, and I have noticed that east coasters are sparing with words, seeming to regard talk as idle frippery, fit only for womenfolk, but even so I never met one as dour as Davie.

He put his head round the kitchen door, and motioned me to rise with a jerk of his thumb. "Ah'm needing a hand at the loading," he said, and was gone.

I worked alongside him loading the wagon, and although I could not match his pace pride drove me on beyond the limits of my strength. By the time the watery sun had lifted over the eastern hill the muscles in my back were shrieking in protest, and I started to flag, snatching sly rests as I dug the fork into the stack, but not having the face to pause openly and take a breather. It would have been different had he been the size of Uilleam Mor, but seeing that wee man toiling tirelessly, and not seeming to put the least effort into his work, I felt my weakness as something shameful and would have dropped in my tracks rather than admit that I was done.

I tried to lure him into talk, but he would have none of it. All I got was nods and grunts. A nod to say yes, the

load of hay was for Seamus Sionnach. A grunt to acknowledge that Uilleam Mor had told him to call at our house
and let my father know that I was working at the inn.
Another grunt to say he would bring back any gear they
had for me. A nod to indicate he expected to be back by
nightfall, followed by a barked, "If we are not all day at
the loading."

He was as good as his word. I was busy polishing the
brass lamps and fittings on Uilleam Mor's gig, in the shed
adjoining the stables, when I heard the rumble of the big
wagon outside. Davie came in, as quick and spry as if the
day was new started and there was no sliver of moon above
the hill to mark the coming of night. He dumped a sail-
cloth bag at my feet and fished a crumpled letter from his
greasy waistcoat. I smoothed it out, and recognised the
Maighstir's neat, cramped hand. Likely enough Davie
would have had to wait while the *cailleach* hurried to the
school to get the *Maighstir* to pen a note. That would not
have pleased him.

But all he said was, "You know him they call Parnell?"

I nodded. Parnell was the nickname of Tormod, a second
cousin of my father, who stayed in Valtos, a township to
the south of our own. He was a bit of a lawyer, fond of big
words and writing letters to the newspapers, but not slow
when it came to speaking up for the people's rights. That
was how he got his nickname, after the great Irish leader,
Parnell.

"Parnell was arrested," Davie said. "He is in the jail in
Portree."

"In the jail? A quiet man like Parnell? For what? He
is handy with his tongue, right enough, but I never heard
tell of a man being put to the jail for speaking out o' turn."

Davie shrugged. "Well, you heard it now, boy. Let it

be a lesson to you. Leave the speaking to the ones that know. Do your work, and sing dumb, and you will never want for a bite or a place to lay your head." And so saying he marched off, leaving me too dazed to marvel at the fact that it was far and away the longest speech I had ever got out of him.

I moved under the hanging lantern, and opened the letter.

"*Dear Alasdair*," I read, and it was queer reading the *cailleach's* words set down in the careful hand of the *Maighstir*. "*I am getting Mr. Nicolson to make this letter for me. Your father and I are well pleased that you have got a start with Mr. Gordon.* (That was a lie. The *bodach* could not stand Uilleam Mor, and was never done calling him the biggest rogue in creation). *Mr. Gordon is well thought of. They say he gifted part of the money for the building of the new kirk in Uig. If you are diligent* (that was one of the *Maighstir's*, for sure; the *cailleach* never spoke that word) *in your work, you may be sure Mr. Gordon will see to your advancement.*

"*The brindle cow was coughing, but is better now. We are all well.*

"*I am sending clothes over by the carrier. There is a new-baked girdle scone on top.*

> *Your loving mother*
> *Murdina Stewart* "

Not a word about the factor and the great job she was so sure he would have waiting for me once he had rushed me off to Edinburgh for a proper schooling. It was Uilleam Mor who was to see to my advancement now, and the same one that busy advancing himself he had barely time to draw breath. I crumpled the letter into a ball, and flung it at the far wall.

A breathless voice from the door said, "Are you wild, Alasdair?"

I swung round. It was Murdina, raindrops beading her fair hair, lips parted in what could have been a half-smile or a need to draw breath. She must have run from the inn, Uilleam Mor roaring why was his gig not ready and waiting at the door.

"Wild?" I said, feeling foolishly exposed the way you always do when you think you are alone and suddenly discover someone watching you. "Ach, no." Her eyes were on the crumpled ball of paper. "It was just a letter," I said. "I was done with it, and I sort of tossed it away."

She stepped lightly over the hard earthen floor until she was standing alongside me under the lantern. Her hair glistened like ripe corn in a good season when the sun is plentiful and the winds gentle and the rain comes in soft, warm showers from the south-west. It hung about her shoulders, caught back with a black band. I wanted to put out my hand and touch the glittering rain drops clinging to that golden hair.

"Listen," she said urgently, eager blue eyes intent upon my face. "Seamus Sionnach is here, in a right rage by the look of him, and it was your name he was putting off his chest the moment he clapped eyes on Uilleam Mor. Would you not like to know what the pair o' them are saying?"

"Aye, but Uilleam Mor hauled me out o' the taproom to get the gig ready. Supposing he is bawling for it, and the ponies not even——"

"Time enough for that," she said, not stopping to hear me out, but catching my arm and pulling me to the door. "Come on."

She ran for the inn, and she was that fleet of foot, despite her hampering skirts, I was hard pressed to keep up with her. She went in by a door at the back that opened into a room with a stone-flagged floor and white-washed walls. There was a lighted candle standing in the middle of a scrubbed deal table, wooden wash tubs stacked against the wall, and a big iron cauldron hanging from a hook over the open fireplace. Murdina picked up the candle-holder, and put a finger to her lips.

She opened what looked like a cupboard door, and I stood and gawked when I saw that there was a wooden stair behind the door; a stair that narrow it would not have afforded an easy passage for many a one only half the girth of Uilleam Mor. Murdina was half-way up the first flight when she realised I was not behind her. She backed down, glancing over her shoulder, the candle flame guttering wildly in the draught, and beckoned me to follow.

The stair twisted and turned. I cracked my head a couple of times against overhanging beams on the sharp turns, but Murdina, who was near as tall as me, never came to grief. I wondered how many times she had been up and down the hidden stair, and for what purpose.

We came out on a short passage. At the far end of the passage a wider stair wound down. There were two doors on the left. She stopped outside the second door, and once again put a finger to her lips. Turning the handle slowly, she opened the door, and motioned me inside.

We were in a bare attic room with a small barred skylight high in the sloping roof. Murdina placed the candle on the dusty floor, and knelt down feeling the floorboards. Her searching fingers delved into a crack. She lifted out a short length of board. Pinpoints of light filtered through from the ceiling below. The light could have come from cracks in an old ceiling, or from holes drilled to enable a hidden listener to hear the better. I wondered if Murdina knew which.

By lying with my head over the gap I could hear what was being said in Uilleam Mor's parlour, although judging by the way he and Seamus Sionnach were roaring at each other I could have listened in comfort from my bed in the loft above the stables.

"How many more times am I to be telling you?" Seamus Sionnach shouted. "The night o' the fire I came flying out o' the school and I got a sight o' that boy full in the light o' the factor's coach. He was hid behind the coach up against the wall o' the school. Why was he not racing to see the fire along wi' the rest? I will tell you for why. Because the bold lad had put a torch to my stacks, and made straight back to the school, as fast as his legs could carry him, hoping to show face at the meeting as innocent as you please. Easy done supposing you are nimble enough to cross the river by the old stepping stones. Good life, it is no distance at all.

"But the flames got a right grip, and the fire was seen before the bold boy could make the school of it. Use your wits, Uilleam! How could he run for the school, and the rest of us swarming out? So he dodged in behind the coach and flattened himself against the wall. Ach, I am telling you, it was himself right enough. Every other rag in the place fit for such an act was sitting there before me at the meeting. It was the boy, I tell you. It is as plain as the nose on your face."

"And amn't I after telling you until I am sick tired of the sound o' my own voice that the boy was at the meeting?" Uilleam Mor roared. "Major Traill had it from the police. The boy was seen, standing on a split new fire pail at the back o' the lobby in the school. One o' the constables was going to remove him, but the sergeant said to let him be, seeing as there might be trouble wi' the crowd that was there if the police were seen laying hands on a boy."

"The police!" Seamus Sionnach scoffed. "Strangers, every single man o' them. One boy is much the same as another to the police. What way do we know the boy they saw was the son o' that rascal Alasdair Rob?"

"There is no mistaking him," Uilleam Mor retorted, "not wi' that thick black thatch of his hanging over his ears like he had never seen the shears in a twelvemonth, and the impudent eye he has on him. It is the eye on him that marks him out, Seamus." There was a tinkle of glasses; the sound of drinks being poured. Silence again. And then a heavy tread pacing the floor; a loud snort. "Trailing around in rags not fit for a tinker the most o' the time; aye, many's the day I have seen the same one at the cattle-sales, ankle-deep in mud and it bucketing down, and himself barefoot, but still an' all that impudent eye on him. And he shows up here in a jacket and trouser that would near have fitted me, big an' all as I am, so that you would have taken him for a guiser if his face had been blacked, and himself looking at me that haughty you would have thought he was wrapped in a plaid o' the Royal Stewart tartan, and come to grant me a favour."

I could have killed Uilleam Mor. As God is my witness, I could have killed Uilleam Mor. I pressed my face down against the gap between the boards, fearful that Murdina would see my flaming cheeks.

"And you gave him work," Seamus Sionnach said, venom in his voice. "When your stacks are burning I will be there for sure to warm my hands at the blaze."

"Oh, he is fit for firing the stacks, the same one," Uilleam Mor said, too quickly for my liking. "But I know what I am about, Seamus."

"Aye, it looks like it," the ground officer said sourly.

"Because I took him on as a stableboy?" Uilleam Mor's

rumbling laugh filled the small attic room. "That was the factor's idea, and it was a smart one, too. We have got the boy here to see what we can get out o' him."

"Ach, he will never let on."

There was a silence. The floorboards creaked; glasses clinked again.

"Well, that is where you need to use your wits," Uilleam Mor said. "I had Iain at him—the young fellow in charge o' the taproom—and Iain is no fool, I am telling you. The boy made out he had no hand in the firing o' your stacks, but he was up to high doh when Iain said it might be the work of a woman. He was not having that at all."

"Well?"

Uilleam Mor's voice was low for once, but I heard every word. "Amn't I after telling you, man? You have got to use your wits. If the boy is dead against the notion that your fire was the work of a woman—and Iain said he very near choked he was that taken aback—you may be sure it was. And I could name you one well able for the job."

They chanted the name together. "Widow MacGregor."

"*Dhia*, yes," Seamus Sionnach said softly, "the mother o' Lachlann Ban, and herself the one who made him what he was, putting him against those in authority from the day she first gave him suck."

"Who else?" Uilleam Mor put in.

"Oh, fit for such work, fit for such work," the ground officer agreed, fairly spitting the words out. "A right trouble-maker that son of hers—an agitator just—and likely herself brooding now that he is away to America, and desperate to spite those who were against him. Good grief, amn't I the clown not to have seen it long since, and the widow's croft marching wi' that o' my neighbour. She could

68

have slipped over no bother and put a torch to my stacks and not a living soul any the wiser. A man can be too trusting just. But I will hand it to you, Uilleam, you are not slow when it comes to the bit."

"Aye, and we will not be slow in dealing wi' the Widow MacGregor," Uilleam Mor said. "The factor is away to Portree to get the law moving. Sheriff Officer MacDonald will be out to-morrow to evict her for non-payment o' rent, and poind her goods and cattle. The factor says it will serve as a lesson for the rest of them wi' the rent collection due on Monday. Right enough, it will fairly sort them. They will come running wi' the rent—arrears an' all—when they see the Widow MacGregor cleared out o' the place and every scrap of her gear seized."

"She has good cattle beasts," Seamus Sionnach said, the gloom in his voice sounding clear through the ceiling. He would be near weeping at the thought of his brimming stackyard reduced to ashes, at a time when there were beasts within his grasp to be had dirt cheap, and himself without the feeding for them.

"A shame they burned your stacks, Seamus," Uilleam Mor said. "You will be hard pressed to see your own beasts through the winter, far less take on more stock. But the widow's croft is fine and handy to your own. You will be able to work it no bother, and you may be sure the estate will be looking for a tenant who is able to meet the rent. Supposing the widow did fire your stacks, it is yourself will be laughing before you are done."

There was the scrape of a chair; the sound of one of them getting to his feet. "Aye, well, I had best make for home," Seamus Sionnach said. "A man cannot rest easy when there is wicked work o' this sort on the go, and I would not trust my boys to guard a copper farthing, never mind the load o' hay you sent over. As like as not they will be away fooling wi' girls the minute my back is turned."

There was no mistaking Uilleam Mor's heavy tread; the protesting boards telegraphed their message. "Well, a glass to warm you for the road, Seamus. That will——"

Something hard was digging into my back. It was the toe of Murdina's boot. She was on her feet, beckoning urgently to me, lips pursed in a warning to be silent.

I replaced the loose board, and Murdina led the way out of the attic room and down the narrow, twisting stair. She stopped on the last flight and motioned me to wait. I watched her open the stair door a crack and listen carefully, and I wondered what she would do if there was someone in the room and we were trapped on the stair. But the room was empty, and I hurried down to join her.

She put the candle back on the deal table, and snuffed it, and led me to the door. She stopped at the door, her cool hand holding mine tight. Her hair brushed my cheek as she turned to face me. "Alasdair," she whispered, "what did Uilleam Mor mean when he said they would poind Widow MacGregor's cattle?"

"Seize them," I said. "Have them sold by the sheriff officer, to help pay the arrears o' rent. Poinded cattle are supposed to go to the highest bidder, but it is always worked on the quiet by the ones in the know. You may be sure Uilleam Mor will lay hands on the beasts, and get them for next to nothing."

"What will you do?"

"Make over the hill in the night, and warn the *cailleach*," I answered, the words coming as natural as breathing, no thought behind them at all. "Get her beasts put away where the sheriff officer will never find them."

"You will do that for the *cailleach*?"

"Aye, me. Who else is there?"

She was silent, and I said, "Murdina, tell me something."

"What?"

"Is it right that I have an impudent eye on me?"

She was silent again, but I was made bold by the dark and the scent of her hair close to my face and the touch of her hand on mine, and I said, "Well, is it?"

"You have brown eyes," she said, "and I am not for complaining about the look in them."

She lifted the latch and pushed me out. "Quick," she urged—and if she had not made a move I believe I would have stood fast even supposing a score of Uilleam Mors were bearing down on me—"or you will have Himself roaring for his gig."

She ran, fleet-footed, for the kitchen door. I watched her go the whole length of the long white inn before I started for the stables.

6

Uilleam Mor roared right enough, bellowing my name as if I had done him an injury and he was calling me to justice. But I was ready for him, his ponies—and they were a beauty of a pair, dark cream garrons with the same black eel stripe along their strong backs; split twins save for the white hind hoof on one of them—harnessed to the shining gig.

I brought the gig round to the front of the inn where he was waiting, impatient for off, standing plumb beneath the lantern that lit the entrance to the wide porch. I held the garrons by their bridles, keeping my face hidden behind their heads, fearful of what Uilleam Mor might see in my eyes. But he was too busy heaving his great belly into the gig—and that was no easy task, I am telling you—to spare me a glance.

"You fairly took your time, boy," he growled, the springs creaking loud as he settled into his seat. "Away to the taproom, there is plenty work waiting you there." He dragged on the reins, and the spirited garrons tossed their heads, starting away that fast I had to leap clear to avoid being run down.

The path from the inn branched into twin forks to join the road. Uilleam Mor took the south fork, heading the gig up the brae. I wondered if he was away to Portree to join his crony the factor.

"Portree?" Iain Dubh said, the clamour in the packed taproom shredding his voice to a whisper. "Not him. This is the night he visits his friend in Snizort." His watchful eyes circled the crowded room. He put his lips to my ear, the brimming copper measure rock steady in his hand, and gave me a sly wink. "The widow of a sea-captain, they say, wi' two husbands coffined, and herself eager to secure a third." He was killing himself laughing, but he never spilled a drop of drink. I watched him tip the measure expertly into a glass, his restless eyes on the prowl again. "You will be sleeping, boy," he said, "before the gig is back to-night."

The dark fellow's words came back to me hours later as I climbed the ladder to the loft, my head thick with the fumes and the heat and the noise of the taproom, limbs bone-weary and aching for rest. Indeed, his words had never been out of my mind all night, but I had stowed them away, not wanting to bite on them until I had time to think in peace.

Squatting cross-legged on the straw pallet, the lantern glowing bright on the floor beside me, I wondered what to do. I untied the bag the *cailleach* had sent over, and took out her girdle scone. It was tough and leathery, not like the girdle scones of Old Kirsty, the cook, that fairly melted in your mouth and left you near eating your fingers. The *cailleach* had never been much of a hand at girdle scones, and my departure had not improved her any. The black cat came out from his bed in the hay, and arched his back, rubbing himself against my legs. I fed him the most of the scone, and thought and thought until my head started to throb.

If Uilleam Mor was going to be late back, I dare not make over the hill to our township until he had put in an appearance. Sure enough, he would be roaring for me to stable the ponies the minute he was back, and if I was not there when he came, how could I explain my absence? And if the night was near done before he showed up, I would not have sufficient time to get over and back before Sandy the coachman was shouting at me to rise. Either way, that was me in big trouble. And yet I had to warn Lachlann Ban's mother so that she could get her cattle well hidden before the sheriff officer showed face in the township. But how? How?

I smote my fist into my palm. Clown that I was! I was sitting above the answer! It was right there in the stables below. All I had to do was make off with one of the ponies, and do the journey at a fast clip on horseback. Even supposing Uilleam Mor was as late in returning as the dark fellow made out, once he was safely abed, it should be easy enough to get clear with a pony and be there and back before dawn.

But supposing Iain Dubh had been having me on about the weekly trip to Snizort? Supposing he and Uilleam Mor were sitting in the gig at this very moment, lurking in the shadows, waiting to pounce the moment I made off? I was getting fanciful. That was nonsense. Uilleam Mor had no means of knowing that I had overheard him tell Seamus Sionnach that the factor was going to evict Lachlann Ban's mother in the morning.

And why should Iain Dubh lie to me? Right enough, he had tried to find out, at his master's bidding, what I knew about the burning of the ground officer's stacks, but I did not see the hand of Uilleam Mor in the Snizort story. If the innkeeper knew that Iain Dubh was making mock of him behind his back that would be the dark fellow down the road, and himself fortunate if he escaped with his skin whole.

Uilleam Mor was not slow in mocking others, but he would be the first to get wild if he suspected his servants of talking free behind his back. My cheeks burned as I thought of the way he had spoken of me to Seamus Sionnach—and Murdina there beside me taking it all in. I had some score to settle with Himself and the factor. If I lived to be burdened with years, I would never forget the way the two of them had used me, and worse, how I had been clown enough to be taken in by them. Murdina must have thought me a right fool.

The cat settled down on the pallet beside me, purring hard. I stroked him absently, thinking of Murdina and the fellow with the golden beard she had met behind the peat stack. In truth, I did not much fancy the thought of her meeting a man who went about with rings in his ears. I had heard tell of fishermen in the Outer Isles wearing earrings, but I had never seen one. The old men said it was hard on the eyes working at the mending of the nets, and that gold in the ears had saved many a man's sight, although how that could be I knew not. It was strange that I had never got a word out of Murdina about the bearded fellow. And it was to-night he was coming. *I will wait for an hour after the last one is away*, he had said. By the last one he must have meant the last patron to leave the inn. It was a good half-hour since Iain Dubh had cleared the taproom, but some of them would hang about for long enough outside, talking and arguing the toss, before they finally drifted home, like so much flotsam on a slow running tide.

What was he up to? Perhaps he knew that this was the night Uilleam Mor made his weekly trip to Snizort. If Ailean Mor was right, it was the golden-bearded fellow who had fired the ground officer's stacks. But who could believe Ailean Mor, himself half blind, shunning the company of men, and stinking of goat; an old man who saw visions and was fool enough to speak of what he saw? Right enough, there had been prophets in olden times who had seen visions.

It was written so in the Bible. Could it be that Ailean Mor was a prophet, and the rest of us too blinded by the stink of goat to see him for what he was? Well, that was as maybe, but if I had to wait for the innkeeper's return there was no reason why I should not keep an eye open for the bearded one.

I put out the light, and waited in the dark, hearing the rain beating soft on the thick thatch, and the throbbing purr of the cat under my hand. I was that dead tired I would have been asleep in an instant if I had stretched out on the pallet, and for a moment I was sore tempted. I wondered, long after, how my life would have gone had I yielded, but there is no profit in trying to unpick the weft and warp of the years.

What spurred me to my feet was the sudden thought— and I had been slow in coming to it—that the bearded one might be on his way to fire Uilleam Mor's stacks. A flame cunningly kindled in the dry heart of a stack would soon take hold and burn with a fury that the rain would never douse. And if the stacks went up in flames, that was me for the jail, supposing Uilleam Mor did not squeeze the life out of me the minute he got me cornered. I shot down the ladder, lifted the latch on the heavy stable door, and slipped out into the night.

I stood under the great stone lintel in the deep doorway, the walls on either side of me a good five feet thick. Flattened against the drystone wall, eyes and ears alert for the least sight or sound, I made my way round to the gable end of the stables. From the gable I could command a view of Uilleam Mor's stackyard—crammed with a full score of fat stacks of hay and corn—the long lines of his peat stacks, and the inn. There was a light burning at an upper window; everything else in darkness; no sound but the soughing of the wind in the trees between the path and the road, and the steady brush of the rain on the thatched roof of the stables.

I was in the lee of the wind, and the overhanging thatch sheltered me from the rain, except for the drips that fell. As my eyes grew accustomed to the dark, I could make out the shape of the trees, the line of the road winding up the hill, and the dark outline of the new kirk above the inn. The light at the upper window went out. The inn was in darkness. There was not a sight or a sound of a living soul. The cry of a seabird echoed about the cliffs above the bay; a terrible chill cry to be heard in the dark of night, and I could see why in olden times they were thought to bear the souls of dead mariners. Somewhere along the shore, a dog howled. The wind gusted in from the south-west, driving across the open bay and moaning among the trees. It eddied about the stables, spattering my face with rain.

He must have been sheltering under the trees. If he had not kicked a stone as he darted across the path, I doubt if I would have spotted him. He was crouched forward, running for the inn. I wondered if he had a tryst with Murdina—and the thought was like ashes in my mouth—if she was waiting behind a door for his coming.

He stopped some yards from the inn, seeming to fall forward, and for a moment I thought I had lost sight of him. But he rose again, went down once more, straightened to his full height for no longer than it would take me to blink an eye—and vanished! Aye, as sure as I am here, he vanished! It was as if the ground had swallowed him up. Well, I am telling you, supposing Uilleam Mor's stacks— the full score of them—had burst into flames at that moment, I could not have moved a muscle. I stood there petrified, my mind teeming with pictures of Ailean Mor, his sightless eye close to my face, saying, *I saw the coming o' the stranger wi' the bright ring o' gold in his ear,* and Murdina, her hand shielding her eyes, her voice a mocking echo of mine own: *The fellow with the beard? You must have been dreaming, Alasdair. Or seeing a ghost.*

Dhia, was it a ghost I had seen? My mouth was suddenly dry; my heart started to slam in my breast. I strained my eyes, focusing on the spot where I had last seen him. Nothing. He had vanished, right enough.

Maybe I had never seen him at all. Maybe I had been imagining things in the dark; sleeping on my feet, and dreaming perhaps, the sort of feverish dream that often comes when you are bone weary and sleep catches you unawares. But no, I had heard the stone he dislodged as he crossed the path. As God is above, I had seen *something* in the shape of a man, on that I would take my oath.

The wind was rising, gusting strong across the bay and moaning through the trees, plucking at the thatched roof of the stables and swirling around the gable end where I stood flattened back against the wall. I started, as an empty pail was swept away and went clattering across the paved yard at the back of the inn. The night that had been so quiet was suddenly alive with noise. There was a muffled thud of iron on wood; likely a skylight left open and caught by the wind. One of the maids would lose a pretty penny out of her pay if the glass smashed. Sure enough, I was near certain I heard the tinkle of breaking glass above the noise of the wind and the rain.

I stood there against the gable wall, shivering with the cold and wet, never taking my eyes from the place where I had last seen him. How long I stood there, I do not know. I was too numbed—numbed in the mind as well as the body —to mark the passage of time. Indeed, he had risen from the ground and was running for the shelter of the trees—

had vanished into their midst—before I could will my limbs to move, and then it was only to take an uncertain step forward. I stopped again, eyes strained on the clump of trees, watching and listening, heedless of the rain that beat about me.

Slowly, step by laggard step, I advanced towards the spot where he had first disappeared. When I reached the dark hole in the ground, I stood looking down at it for long enough, like one bemused, as if I was witnessing a miracle, and it simple enough in all conscience.

The hole led down to the cellar of the inn. The heavy iron trapdoor that covered the entry was laid back on its hinges. I could see the start of the two sloping beams down which the barrels and kegs were lowered when fresh supplies were unloaded. There were cross supports let into the beams making a ladder down into the cellar. I started down—but slow, that slow you would have taken me for an old man without trust in his limbs, fearful of falling. I was not well up in years, or afraid of coming off the ladder, but I am telling you I had no fancy at all to descend into that black pit.

I stopped on the sixth rung, and listened. There was the sound of running water all around, like the gushing of many springs flowing strong. It was near eight years since the night of the great flood, when the river changed course and the laird's lodge was swept away and the burial ground gave up its dead and open coffins floated in the bay and many a whitened skeleton moved with the tide on the shore. Surely I was not hearing a dark echo from that Sabbath night of flood eight years ago? I scrambled up the ladder, and ran to the stables for a lantern.

The wind put it out on me, but I went on down. My ears had not deceived me; I heard the sound of running water as soon as I got my head below ground away from the noise of the wind. The fumes of liquor were terrible strong in the confined space of the cellar after the clean air above ground. I splashed down on the flagstones. The floor was awash. I could feel the wet coming over the tops of my boots, soaking my feet. I fumbled for a match, and lit the lantern.

The cellar was a wreck. It was not water that was running free but a sea of whisky, rum, wine and porter, gallon upon gallon of it, spilling from the shattered casks and kegs and pouring on to the floor. I splashed through the flood of liquor to the door. It was locked. Holding the lantern on high, I inspected the long lines of wooden racks. Every cask and keg had been staved in, jeroboams of wine overturned and smashed. The sound of running liquid had stilled; the pouring slowed to a trickle. The wealth of Uilleam Mor's cellar was squandered on the floor, seeping away between the cracks in the flagstones.

I had one last look round and splashed towards the trap-door. With a hand on the sloping beams, I started to climb. I had reached the fourth rung when I looked up. There was a face in the gap above, peering down at me. Maybe I was stupid with shock, but I did not realise at once that it was the face of Uilleam Mor. For what seemed an eternity, but could have been only seconds by the count of a clock, we stared at each other. Neither of us uttered a word. But he was the first to move. The heavy iron trapdoor crashed down over the opening, and I was blinded by a shower of dirt and dust.

7

Blinking the dirt out of my eyes, I went on up the ladder. The lantern lit the studded underside of the iron trapdoor, and the square of great black interlocking roof beams it fitted so neat. The two massive bolts that secured it from within were drawn back as far as they could go, and I wondered stupidly how the cellar door came to be locked when the iron trap must have been opened from the inside.

There was not a sound from above, although that was not much to go by. An army could have been on the march nearby without me being any the wiser. The heavy trapdoor, fitting so snug, was as good as a dungeon wall in sealing off all sound above ground.

The clang of something hard and heavy dropping on the iron of the trapdoor rang out so sharp and sudden I very near let go of the lantern. Flakes of rust and dirt showered down on me. I backed down the ladder, tense and wary as a cornered fox, nerves so on edge I started at the movement of my own shadow.

Silence again. This time the silence endured. I climbed slowly up the ladder, and listened, an ear against the cold iron. Not a sound. Moving up to the topmost spar, I got my shoulder against the trapdoor, spread my feet wide securing a firm purchase where the spar joined the sloping beams, and heaved—heaved with all the strength I could summon from that awkward perch. The trap did not budge.

I scrambled down the ladder, and ran to the door at the far end of the cellar. Perhaps I had been mistaken; the door might be stiff to open. I twisted the handle, and flung myself against the stout door. It never moved. The cellar door was securely locked. Hardly knowing what I was doing, I stumbled back to the ladder, and climbed it once more. Perched on the top rung, the lantern clutched in my left hand, I strove in a frenzy of fear to lift the trapdoor, heaving and straining at the studded iron until my heart was near bursting and coloured lights danced before my eyes. Try as I might, I could not shift it an inch. The iron trapdoor could have been bolted to the beam for all the impression I made on it.

Dizzy and spent, I moved a few rungs down the ladder, resting my back against it, one arm hooked around a spar. I was still sprawled there, gasping for breath, when the cellar door was flung open.

Uilleam Mor rushed in—and stopped short. He could not have halted any quicker if he had found himself poised on the edge of the cliff at Valtos, facing a sheer drop to the rocks hundreds of feet below. Behind him, each of them bearing a lantern, stood Iain Dubh and Mata Caogach, a squint-eyed fellow, barrel-chested and long in the arm, who did the heavy work about the place and was always on hand to put a stop to fights in the taproom.

Uilleam Mor beckoned to them to raise their lanterns high. He had spotted me the moment he came in the door, but he could not lift his eyes from the floor, awash with his good liquor. His gaze crawled around the wrecked cellar. The silence and the stillness of him had me quaking. I eased myself stealthily up another rung on the ladder, braced for the ear-splitting roar that was bound to come any moment now.

But not a sound issued from his lips. As sure as I am here, not a sound issued from the lips of Uilleam Mor. He just gave his head a quick shake, like a swimmer surfacing, and started forward slowly, so slowly you would have thought he was walking behind a coffin on the solemn march to the burial ground. The only sound was the splashing strides the three of them made as they moved through the sea of liquor on the floor.

Uilleam Mor walked like an old, drunk man, legs splayed wide, broad back that bent you could have believed he carried a boll of meal across his shoulders. He stopped at the foot of the ladder, and put out a hand, supporting himself against one of the sloping beams. I thought for sure he was drunk, seeing the way he swayed and his head stayed sunk deep on his chest.

But not when he looked up at me, not then. He was not drunk, not him, unless a man can be drunk with hate. In the light of the lanterns, his face was the colour of dry clay. It was glazed with sweat. His mouth was open, spittle dribbling free down his chin, and his breath came in hard, grunting gasps, as if it was an agony for him to take air into his lungs. His small eyes never wavered from my face, and I swear they gleamed an evil pink in the lamplight, like the eyes of a ferret thirsting for blood.

There was not a sound in the cellar save the slow gentle drip from the broken casks and shattered jeroboams: that, and the rasping, terrible hard breathing of Uilleam Mor. The lantern bearers at his back might have been turned to stone they stood that still. So might I, for that matter, stiffened back against the ladder, held rigid in the baleful stare of those hot, blood-lusting eyes.

And it was out of the silence and stillness that he sprang. He sprang—despite the great belly on him—with the mur-

derous speed of a hunter whose patience has burst its bonds
he is that desperate eager for the kill. His fingers fastened
on my ankle. I tried to kick clear, but there was no denying
the grip he had on me. My lantern went flying, and smashed
on the floor. I was jerked off the ladder, and landed on my
back with a thump that drove the breath from my body,
and drenched the three of them in a spray of liquor.

He was on to me before I could start to struggle to my
knees, clawing hands bunching the front of my jersey as he
hauled me to my feet. I saw his great fist draw back to
strike, and I tried to put up my hands to save my face. It
was as well for me to have attempted to fend off the blow
of a weighted club. His fist brushed through my guard and
smashed into my face. White-hot pain seared my nose. I
felt the blood welling in my mouth and throat as I crashed
back over a broken barrel, and I cried out as a splintered
stave jabbed into the small of my back, sharp as a knife-
thrust.

He plucked me off the flooded floor as if there was no
more weight in my bones than a bag of chaff, heedless of the
blood that gushed from my nose and splashed across his
hands, soiling his white cuffs. Little bubbles of foam flecked
the corners of his mouth. His narrowed eyes were shot with
blood. He drew back and swung at me again. I tried to
duck the blow, and it caught me flush on the left ear. My
head seemed to explode, and I found myself stretched flat
on my back in the wet. The blood was running down my
throat, near choking me, and my face seemed to be on fire,
I tried to lift my head, and was blinded by a flood of stinging
liquid.

Uilleam Mor was standing over me, kicking the liquor into
my face. "Drink!" he was shouting. "Drink! Drink!
until you choke, you misbegotten spawn o' the Devil."

I rolled over, but before I could push myself up he had seized me by the hair and yanked me to my feet. He tugged savagely at my hair until I was arched back gazing up into his maddened face. I cried out in desperation, "It was not me smashed the cellar."

He swung me round to face him, his bloodstained hands shifting to my throat. "Not you?" he said, the words drifting to me through a blaze of pain, crooned that soft I wondered if my hearing was gone. His face swam before my eyes; a sweating, crazed, demented mask of a face. There was murder in his eyes. "Not you," he crooned. "You only came along wi' a lantern to take a look." His voice rose to a scream of fury. "Or maybe you were sleep-walking just?"

His big hands tightened on my throat, squeezing hard. I beat at his chest. It was like striking a solid wall of rock. The last thing I remember was his face seeming to swell before my eyes. It floated above me, bloated and huge, stifling me in spreading rolls of sweating flesh. The lanterns spun madly, and everything went black.

I did not know whether I was alive or dead, and that is the truth of it. Everything was black, shrouded in a silence as deep as the grave. Heaven could not be black, I told myself, and no preacher I had ever heard was for making out the other place to be a haven of quiet. I puzzled over the problem for long enough, foolish as that may seem.

As my head cleared, and memory flooded back, I was caught in a new apprehension. I was afraid, afraid of being suddenly seized again, and battered and throttled once more. I held my breath, listening with every nerve of my being strained to catch the least sound. There was not a murmur, not so much as the softest intake of breath. I was

alone. Slowly, like an infant learning a new trick, I opened
my clenched fists and flexed my fingers. My hands touched
dry boards. It was not the floor of the cellar, that was a
sure thing. The stink of liquor was something terrible, but
it came from my sodden clothes.

I sat up, and a thousand fiery needles sprang to life, every
one of them hard on the go piercing my skull. I sat motionless, afraid to so much as blink an eye until the thousand
stabbing points of fire had dulled to a throbbing pain that
did not make the twitch of an eyelid an agony. I put up
a hand and drew my fingertips lightly across my nose and
mouth. My face felt out of shape, the swollen upper lip
pushing my nose awry, and it strangely thickened. My hand
came away wet and sticky. I wiped it on my sodden trouser,
not fancying the feel of blood, even if it was mine own.

The stink from my soaking clothes was turning my
stomach. I got to my knees, and retched. My mouth was
bitter with the taste of blood, my throat that sore it was as if
Uilleam Mor's great hands were still clamped tight about
my windpipe. Try as I may, I could not swallow. When I
passed my dry tongue about my swollen, blood-caked lips
I brought on another fit of retching.

I crawled forward on my hands and knees. Two painful
paces and I was up against a wall. I turned about, and
headed in the opposite direction. Eight short hand paces
and I had reached the other wall. I moved along it until
I came to a corner, then turned about, still on my hands and
knees, and measured the length of the wall. Seven paces.
I pushed myself upright, straightening slowly, and cracked
my head on the roof, setting the burning needles to work
again. I groped for the roof with my hands. It sloped
steeply upwards. I walked to the opposite wall, crossed
hands guarding my head from any obstacles, and felt my

way along the wall until I came to the door. I tried the handle. The door was locked.

Satisfied—and if the truth be told too spent to take another step—I sank to the floor. Sitting with my back to the door, mouth clamped tight shut, I fought off wave after wave of sickness. At least, I knew now where I was. In a locked attic room, and one much the same size as the room where Murdina and I had listened in on Uilleam Mor.

Twice I searched the floor for the loose board—certain sure I had covered every inch of the flooring—and twice it eluded my prying fingers. But I tried a third time, and I had no sooner started feeling over the floor than my fingers delved into a deep crack, and up came the loose board. Light filtered through from the tiny holes in the ceiling below, but although I lay with my head over the gap I could not hear a sound.

I think I must have dozed off because I started in alarm when a door shut. Uilleam Mor's voice sounded directly below. "You boys will be the better of a quick dram before you make back to your beds. I could not bide easy until we had been over every room in the place, and seen there was nothing amiss in the stables, and the stacks were safe. Good grief, that boy was fit to fire the inn over our heads, supposing he took the notion."

"Aye, fit for it, the same one." It was Iain Dubh, eagerly echoing his master. He said something I did not catch, and Uilleam Mor cried, "Not him. He stays here until Saturday, where no lawyer can get near him, and help him spin a web o' lies. Come Saturday the bold boy can talk to his heart's content, but I doubt he will not be so eager to use his tongue when he sees who he has to face. Ach well, I will not be the only one to rest easier o' nights once that boy is put behind bars, and it will be many a long day before he is free to roam again, you may be sure o' that."

The boards groaned under Uilleam Mor's heavy tread. The light went out below, and the door slammed. I slid the loose board gently into place, and curled up on the floor, my head cradled on my arm.

It is queer how the mind is often more composed when the body has been tried beyond endurance and is altogether spent. If I had been in my usual trim I would have worried myself sick wondering who Uilleam Mor had coming to see me on Saturday, and why he had not handed me over to the police. But I never gave it a thought.

In my mind's eye, I could see the iron trapdoor in the cellar—would I ever forget it?—the bolts drawn, and the door of the cellar locked. Someone had unlocked that door and unbolted the trap ready for the entry of the bearded one, and slipped away again by the cellar door, locking it behind them. That someone must be Murdina, and if Uilleam Mor had done the rounds of the inn, it was a sure thing he would have been giving me my character for all to hear. So Murdina must know that I was held in the inn, blamed for the wrecking of the cellar, and she was not the one to stand idly by and see me falsely accused. Surely, if the bearded one had nerve enough to fire the stacks of Seamus Sionnach and wreck Uilleam Mor's cellar, the same one could be relied upon to get me out of the inn before Saturday. I shut my eyes on that thought, and my aching body surrendered to sleep.

She was inside the room and kneeling on the floor beside me before I woke. "*Ist!*" she whispered, putting a finger to her lips.

There was a lighted candle beside her. She held it up

to see me the better. The flame guttered wildly as she put it down again. Her hand was shaking.

"What is it?" I said. She had no need to hush me. The only voice I could muster was a hoarse whisper that could not have been heard at the other side of the room.

"Your face," she said, and she was weeping, the tears running free down her cheeks. "Oh, Alasdair, Alasdair, your poor face."

"You should have seen the face on Uilleam Mor," I said, struggling to sit up, and not finding it easy, "when he saw his cellar floating in drink."

"I saw Mata Caogach and Iain Dubh carrying you up the stair," she whispered, "and I thought he had killed you." She blinked back the tears, and tried to scrub her cheeks dry with the back of her hand. "Oh, Alasdair, what were you doing in the cellar after saying you were for making over the hill to warn them of the coming o' the sheriff officer?"

"I saw the bearded fellow, and I was wondering what he was at."

"He was at the wrecking o' the cellar," she said, in a fierce whisper, as if she had sensed the smouldering resentment behind my words, "and it was myself saw to it that the trap-door was open for him." She bit her lip, her eyes flooding with tears. I waited for her to go on, but she rose to her feet, drawing her long black cloak about her. "Do you think you can walk?" she said, distant as a stranger all of a sudden.

"Aye, fine." I was swept by an unreasoning surge of anger. "It would take more than a bloodied nose to put me on my back, girl."

But for all my bold words I was glad enough of the support of her arm when I got to my feet. She snuffed the candle and took my hand, and it was as well for me that she led the way at a snail's pace or I fear my legs would have given under me.

It was different once we got clear of the inn. The rain had stopped, the clear night sky glittering thick with stars, making dark fortresses of the towering headlands and casting a shimmer of light on the black peak of Beinn Edra. The cold night air struck chill on my wet clothes, but it was meat and drink to me after the airless attic room, and when I clapped eyes on the winding ribbon of road the strength came back to my limbs something wonderful.

She had tethered one of Uilleam Mor's dark cream garrons—the one with a white hind hoof—in the trees below the path. She took the pony by the bridle and led him through the trees and across the drain to the road. Once we were on the road she quickened her pace, and she did not stop or utter a word until we had crossed the new iron bridge over the river. I glanced up the road at the factor's house. There was not a light to be seen, but that did not make me any the happier. She had some nerve on her, Murdina. You would never catch me dallying on the factor's doorstep. I would not have stopped until we were on the high moor, and the factor would have needed wings to get near us.

She thrust the bridle into my hands. "Away you go, Alasdair," she said, "and mind you keep clear o' the police. Uilleam Mor will have them hunting you once he finds you have flown."

"Look, Murdina," I said, catching her arm as she turned to go, "you cannot go back to the inn. How long before Uilleam Mor finds out that you——"

"I am not for going back," she cut in coolly.

"But where——"

"He will never follow where I am going." If she was not smiling, there was a smile in her voice.

"But when will I see you? How——"

"I will see you," she said, as if no more than a turf dyke was to separate us.

"How do you know?"

"I know." She took my hand in both of hers. "Make haste. You have got to warn the widow of the coming of the sheriff officer."

She let go of my hand, and I clambered awkwardly on to the pony's broad back. She had not saddled him, but I was well accustomed to riding bareback. That was the way we always brought the ponies home when they had been ranging on the hill.

"Take care, Alasdair," she said, and was gone, running swiftly across the bridge. She took the path past the mill leading to the shore. I watched her until she was lost among the trees, wondering if the bearded one was waiting for her in the shadows.

I parted company with the garron a mile or so from our township, and did the rest of the journey on foot, coming on to the widow's croft from the south, and so avoiding Seamus Sionnach's land. I knew fine her door would not be bolted, but I knocked just the same, not wanting to walk in and give her a fright. She must have been a light sleeper, because I heard her step after the second knock. "Who is there?" she called from behind the closed door, and it was not like the widow to be slow in opening up.

"It is me—Alasdair," I said, hoping she could hear my hoarse whisper. "I have news for you."

She let me in, and I groped my way to the bench, the warm peat reek of the kitchen welcoming as the soft folds

of a thick plaid. Once I had taken the weight off my feet
I felt I could never rise again this night unaided.

"Wait you," she said, "I will get the lamp going." She
sniffed. "*Dhia*, boy, have you been at the whisky?"

"Not me," I said. "It is my clothes just. They got soaked
in the stuff."

She got the lamp lit, and held it up, peering down at me.
"Well, well," she said, as calm as you please, "is this you
back from the wars, boy?"

"That was the work of Uilleam Mor," I said, feeling my
face, and it terrible strange to the touch, "and the same one
has plans to thieve your cattle. The sheriff officer is to be
over this day wi' orders to evict you and poind your beasts.
We will need to get them clear o' the place before dawn, or
you may be sure Seamus Sionnach will be marking their
passage. There is not——" I stopped, conscious of eyes
other than the widow's on me. I swung round. A man was
standing in the deep doorway from the byre. For a moment
I thought I was seeing things, but as he came forward into
the light it was plain that he was of solid flesh and bone.

The burden of struggling alone that had so oppressed me
was shed entirely in that instant of recognition. I was on
my feet in a flash, and the hoarse croak that escaped my
lips would have been a glad cry of joy if only my throat
had been working right. "Lachlann Ban!" I cried.

8

He pushed me down on the bench, stemming the flood of questions that burst from my lips with a quick lift of his hand—and when Lachlann Ban commanded I had no thought but to obey. Mind you, it was good to rest easy and have true friends waiting on me.

The *cailleach* rummaged in a chest for dry clothes, while Lachlann Ban fed fresh peats to the slumbering fire and quickened it into a bright blaze. The kettle was soon spouting steam and the widow got to work with a basin of water and a soft cloth, gently bathing the caked blood from my face. What with the freshening touch of the wet cloth, and the crisp feel of dry clothes on my back, and a bowl of brose warming my belly, I was all set to sit up the rest of the night listening to Lachlann Ban. But it was me who had to do the talking. He wanted to know everything that had happened from the moment I had first seen the flames rising from Seamus Sionnach's burning stacks.

He never said a word during the telling, and he was silent when I got to the end of my tale, sitting bent low on the birch-bough stool by the fire, his chin cupped in his hands. The leaping peat fire flames burnished the thick thatch of his straw coloured hair, flushing his tanned face so that the long pale scar on his left cheek made a stark furrow of white on the weathered skin. He had got thinner, all the planes of his face sharpened, so that in repose he seemed to be all bony strength, as if his countenance had been cleft from rock.

He was not a big man, Lachlann Ban—shorter than my father, and the *bodach* was not big—but there was such a strength and power in the very step and bearing of him that you never noticed his lack of inches, and it always came as a surprise to discover that men you had thought to be much smaller than him were really a good head higher. I knew fine the power that was in him, but I had never sensed it more strongly than at this moment, and himself motionless by the fire, that still a stranger might have taken him to be sleeping.

I had no idea what he would say when I was done telling my story, although—if the truth be told—I would not have been surprised if he had slipped in a word or two of praise for me, and for sure I expected him to lay into Uilleam Mor with a cursing strong enough to burn his ears at a distance of miles. Indeed, the *cailleach* had not been slow to seize on the innkeeper's name. When I had told how he had near strangled me in the cellar, she had rolled his name off her tongue as if it was an abomination to her, and spat her contempt into the fire. Lachlann Ban had stayed silent. And all he said now was: "You thought you were alone, eh?"

"Well, so I was," I said, that puzzled I did not know what to make of his words.

"The girl? Was the girl not with you?"

"Aye, Murdina," I said, and then, not wanting to look as if I was claiming credit that was her due. "Murdina did well. She had some nerve on her for a girl."

"She gave you a good hand. You said so yourself. You said if it had not been for the girl you would never have got clear of the inn."

"Aye, that is right enough."

"And what of those without land scraping a living down on the shore below the inn, the most o' them folk cleared from their land in Glenuig to make a rich tack for Uilleam Mor? You had them at your back, boy. They were with you, not Uilleam Mor. A word to them that you were held prisoner, and they would have had you out o' the inn and away for sure."

I made to speak, but he rushed on, "And supposing he had killed you? *Dhia*, Alasdair, your name would ha' been on the lips o' thousands away in Glasgow—aye, and in Chicago and New York, too!—every one o' them, Scots and Americans, demanding justice for you and an end to the rule o' the laird and the factor and the tacksman."

"Good grief, Lachlann," I croaked, "are you for making out I would ha' been better dead?"

He got to his feet, laughing that hard he had to hold his sides. "No, boy, you are better living," he said, the laughter still bubbling in his throat. "All I am saying is that you were not alone." He started to pace the floor, the words spilling fast from his lips now that he was on the go. "It is that wolf of a factor who walks alone. Tacksmen, like Uilleam Mor, that sick wi' greed for more land they are not caring supposing hundreds o' good folk are driven to the shore to starve so long as they thrive. And jackals, the like o' Seamus Sionnach, sniffing at the heels o' their masters, hoping there will be pickings when the big fellows are gorged. They are the ones that are alone." He stopped his restless pacing to face me over the fire. "Count them," he urged, holding his hands high—big hands they were for a man of his size, strong hands, schooled and toughened in the work of the *cas-chrom* and the spade and the reaping hook —fingers spread wide. "You are not needing more than the one pair o' hands to mark their number. But see you the host on our side—hundreds just in this one corner; thousands if you carry the count the length of every glen between here and Bracadale, and that is the north end o' the island just. And for every one of us here in the home of our fathers you can count a full score in Glasgow, sons o' the men that were cleared from the land in days gone by, but Highland still, as good at the Gaelic as you and me, and fierce, boy, terrible fierce to defend our rights. Ach, I am telling you, we have the numbers to swamp the factor and his cronies."

"Aye, but the factor has the law at his back," I said. "A message from him on the telegraph, and the police come running, and if the police are not able you know well enough Sheriff Ivory will not be slow in summoning the marines. The law——"

"The law!" he barked, and it was his turn to make the fire sizzle as he spat his contempt. "There is no law in this place. The only law is the will o' the factor, and see you how he has used his will. A skelp o' hill grazing taken from us here, another big bite o' land there, and all the time the rents going up, up, up. What way can a man meet a bigger rent when the grazing land for his beasts is taken from him, and he is that poor off for sustenance just the one bad harvest is enough to bring famine to his door? *Dhia*, we are become like beasts ourselves in this place, that weak the wolf can thin the herd at his ease, and never a fear o' them turning and savaging him. We have forgotten how to strike, boy, because each one of us thinks he stands alone."

"You were after thinking that yourself, Lachlann," I said, and it was the truth, although I hesitated before I put the thought into words, fearful that he might take it on the nose.

"I mind you saying that was why you were clearing off to America, you could not get the rest o' them to stand fast with you."

"And that is why I am back," he cried, flinging his arms wide, the bursting energy within him spilling out in that swift movement. "Amn't I after trying to tell you I have learned my lesson? See you, I got the length o' Glasgow, and I was bound for America. As I am before God, that was the only thought in my head. But I had the address of a man from this place, and I sought him out, knowing he would give me shelter for the night. I mind the place well. It was down a long close." He wrinkled his nose. "I can smell that close yet. It stank like a midden in a hot summer, like a passage underground it was, the tenements climbing that high on either side, and stairs galore to mount before I came to his room. I am telling you, boy, I was afraid to look out of a window he was that high up. But inside his room!—*Dhia*, I could have been home again there were that many tongues on the go, and all of them going at it good style in the Gaelic."

"Aye, but it is not good for a man the city," the *cailleach* said. "A man bred to the heather must have a sight o' sea and loch, and the hills free before him, or he will perish whatever."

"They took me to a meeting on the Glasgow Green," Lachlann Ban went on. "Not a soul in this place has ever seen the like o' that meeting. There were thousands, beyond number. It put me in mind of the words o' the preachers—*a great multitude gathered together*. Aye, that was it just—*a great multitude gathered together*.

"And educated men on the platform mind, one o' them a professor from the university, they said. And every one o' them speaking up for us and our rights. And it was the professor himself—a right professor, mind!—who laid into Sheriff Ivory, telling of the crimes—aye, *crimes*, he said—Ivory had committed against us.

"When the speakers were done, they called from the platform was there anyone there fresh from the islands wi' news of what was doing. Well, I am telling you, the sweat fairly came out on me when I got up on that platform and saw the multitude that was facing me. If I had not had a dram in me, I doubt I would never have had the nerve. Anyway, I spoke up. And that was the start of it, boy."

"How do you mean the start?" I said.

"The start o' me taking the road back. You see, I would still ha' been off to America had not an American halted me and turned me in my tracks."

"Away!"

"Aye, right enough. Mr. Henry George is his name. He is famous, boy, famous. It was himself came over from America to help form the Land Restoration League, for to get back the land that was stolen from us. And it was Mr. George made me see we were not alone. There he was in Glasgow, and himself all the way from America, a big man in the world, a maker of books—aye, he has books to his name, the same one—and himself that taken up with our struggle you would think he had been born and bred in the heather.

" 'Give it a try, Lachlann,' he said to me. 'Get back among your own people and spread the message. Tell them they must join the Land League if they are to find the strength to resist those who would drive them from the land. What is one stone? A child could fling it aside. But take hundreds of stones, lock them fast together, the one supporting the other and adding strength to the whole, and you have a wall that a Samson could not sunder. That is the message you must give them.'

"I said I was not able, that I did not have the schooling for such work. He laughed at me. Aye, right enough, he laughed at me. And I mind well his words. 'A knowledge o' Latin and Greek will not add a single acre to your township,' Mr. George said. 'And it is land that is your problem, Lachlann, not a lack o' Greek and Latin. You know the land, you know the people who live on the land, you know what they need to be able to raise their crops and cattle and provide for their families without fear o' famine stalking them close. And you can take the message to them in their own tongue, which I cannot do.'

"I was still not fancying the idea, not fancying coming back home and them all saying, ach, he was all big talk when it came to the bit, one look at a ship in the Glasgow docks casting off her moorings and he took fright at the thought o' crossing the ocean to America. You know fine the talk they would ha' made. But Mr. George sent me to Wester Ross, and I worked there for the Land League, gathering members and getting them organised strong, so that it was not a poor crofter standing alone in fear that the factors had to tackle but the Land League wi' the like o' Mr. George at its head.

"Then I heard of the death o' the laird and the return o' that rag of a factor, Major Traill." His fingers traced the scar on his cheek. "That was me done wi' Wester Ross, boy. I crossed from Gairloch last Monday in Calum Og's smack, and what did we see when we came ashore but the school blazing wi' lights and the factor's coach at the gates. Calum and me we thought we would make a better blaze for him, and strike at that rogue of a Seamus Sionnach where it would hurt him bad."

"Calum Og," I said, "that is him wi' the fair beard and the ring in his ear?"

"Aye, that is Calum Og," Lachlann Ban said. "A great Land Leaguer, the same one, and little wonder seeing the way his father was treated. Calum's father belonged to Glenuig. The *bodach* fought in the Russian War, and when he came home—and himself near dead wi' the fever—he found his wife and family cast on the shore, and all Glenuig in the hands of Uilleam Mor. The *bodach* is dead long since, but the son has not forgotten.

"Well, I was telling you, after we fired the *Sionnach's* stacks, Calum made back to the smack and sailed for Uig. He was going to see his folk and spread the message o' the Land League around Snizort and Waternish." He smiled one of his rare smiles that banished entire the hard lines from his face. "And you may be sure once Calum Og set foot in Uig he was not for leaving without paying a call at the inn."

"If only I had known what he was about," I said. "If only I had got a whisper you were back, Lachlann. I would——"

"Not a soul knows I am here," he cut in sharply, "not even your father, and I am not for showing face until the day o' the rent collection. That day the factor will be here, and it is him I am waiting for. Supposing he knew I was back he would have police galore at the lodge on the lookout for me, and I am easy seen"—he smiled again, a crooked smile this time, as his forefinger ploughed the long furrow on his cheek—"since he left his mark on me. But it is not me he will be looking for, it is you, Alasdair, and that suits me fine."

"Looking for me?" I said stupidly. "The factor?"

"Aye, Uilleam Mor will be on to him the minute he finds

you gone, wanting a warrant put out for your arrest. They will have you down for the wrecking o' the inn cellar, and the firing o' the stacks, and like as not Uilleam Mor will name you for a horse thief."

"But I turned back the pony," I protested. "That garron would make his own way back to the inn no bother. How can Uilleam Mor name me for a horse thief?"

"How?" Lachlann Ban shrugged. "As well for you to ask how can he breathe. I am telling you, Uilleam Mor is fit for stabling the pony in a quiet corner, and never letting on the beast is back. Fine he knows the law comes down terrible hard on a horse thief."

"But it was not me who fired the stacks," I cried, "nor wrecked the cellar, and all I did was take a loan o' the pony."

"And you think the sheriff wi' the wig and the robes, him wi' the job o' judging, would believe you? You forget, boy, you were the one who was to get a right schooling in Edinburgh to fit you for working along wi' the gentry on the estate. The factor would be on to that. He would make out you were that wild at being given a start in the stables this was you getting your own back."

"So what am I to do? Go quiet to the jail?"

"Never the day, boy. They must lay hands on you first, and it is myself will see they never get near you."

"What way could they get a hold o' you, Alasdair," the *cailleach* said, "and not a policeman able to get within miles but we would have word o' their coming?"

Lachlann Ban clapped me on the shoulder. "Never you fear, Alasdair, when I have sorted that rag of a factor they will not be worrying about you, supposing you had fired a dozen stackyards."

I was not so sure about that. I wished I could be as cool

as Lachlann Ban and his widowed mother. If Sheriff Ivory himself had suddenly appeared in the door it would not have put the pair of them up or down.

"Think of it, boy," Lachlann Ban said softly, looking at me, but not seeing me at all, his eyes on some far distant prospect beyond my ken, "the factor waiting at the lodge, with his clerk at his right hand hungry to scoop in the last penny, and Seamus Sionnach close perched on his left, a ready lie on his lips for those that have beggared themselves to find the rent; the three o' them certain sure they have us all by the throat—and then I walk in."

"But you cannot stay quiet until the rent collection," I burst out. "You are after forgetting the sheriff officer. He is to be here this day to seize your beasts. We had best get them away, and quick."

"Sit you down," he said, as cool as you please. "The cattle stay snug in the byre."

"They will not stay long in the byre once the sheriff officer claps eyes on them," I cried, wild at his indifference, the injustice of it all swamping me in a sudden flood of self pity. You would never think I had risked being named a horse thief, and all to warn his mother, the way Lachlann Ban carried on, that unmoved you could have believed the sheriff officer was only coming to drink tea and talk over old times with the pair of them. "Amn't I after telling you the factor has it all fixed," I said wearily. "The sheriff officer has orders to evict you."

"Not me," he said calmly. "The factor and the rest o' them think I am away to America." He pointed to his mother. "It is herself they are after evicting, not me."

The *cailleach* picked up a peat. She had big, powerful hands, the strength in them mocking the white in her hair. She broke the peat in two and fitted the pieces into the red heart of the fire. "It will be a poor day for me," she said, "when I am needing a hand from Lachlann to put the like o' the sheriff officer from the door."

It was no idle boast she made, you would know that in a moment seeing her sitting there by her own fire, strong and square and unafraid. There were not many in the place the equal of Lachlann Ban's widowed mother, herself as strong as any man, able to make a straight lift of a boll of meal from the ground to her shoulder and carry the burden without flagging, leaving others—aye, and men among them—stumbling in her wake, bent near double. She was more than a match for any man who sought to force her from her own hearth.

I said as much to Lachlann Ban when the two of us were stretched out on a bed of sweet-smelling hay in the byre, the door securely barred, and above our heads a cunningly fashioned trap between the roof beams. Even supposing we were taken unawares, at the first sound of a fist on the door, we could have been through the hidden trap in the roof and out on to the hill at the back of the byre.

"Aye, she is a warrior," he said, yawning. "You can rest easy, boy. The *cailleach* is the one to sort the sheriff officer."

I lay still, my aching bones seeming to melt in the warm nest of hay, the pain dissolving as I drifted close to sleep. It was too good to lose. I struggled to keep awake, listening to the slow, deep breathing of the cattle in their stalls, and the quicker breath of Lachlann Ban beside me. If you have never slept in a byre you can have no idea of the wonderful peace there is in the sound of stalled cattle in the night, breathing slow.

"Lachlann," I said.

"Aye." His voice was a drowsy murmur.

"When you see the factor—at the rent collection, I mean—what will you do to him?"

He grunted, and turned on his side, dragging the blankets off me. "What will you do, Lachlann," I repeated, "when you see the factor?"

"Ach, give him a scare." His voice trailed off into a long drawn-out yawn. He shifted restlessly, tugging at the blankets. "Away to sleep, boy."

Sleep was not long in coming, but it was not speeded any by Lachlann Ban. He was that restless you would have thought he had the fever on him. He kept rolling from side to side, and twice he startled me by suddenly shouting out loud in his sleep. I could not make out the words, but whoever they were aimed at was getting the rough end of his tongue, that was a sure thing. Indeed, he sounded that wild it was a wonder to me he did not strike out with his fists, and I was not fancying a rage so fierce that it could not be stilled by sleep.

I woke once, wondering why I was cold, to find he had stripped me of the blankets. I groped about trying to find an end of blanket, but he had turned over dragging them away with him. My searching hand encountered the end of the rolled coat that served as his pillow, and fastened on something hard. I must have been stupid with sleep, because it was long enough before I realised I was gripping the barrel of a pistol.

If I had been wise I should have hidden the pistol, but at that moment he rolled towards me again, and I had only the one thought in my head. I let go of the pistol and snatched at the blankets with both hands, not caring supposing there was an armoury hidden in the hay so long as I could secure my share of the covers and sleep undisturbed.

9

When I awoke again he was gone, only a flattened hollow beside me in the hay to show that he had slept there. The rolled coat and the pistol had gone with him. I wondered if I had imagined it all, if the feel of the pistol—and I could trace its shape from the smooth barrel to the studded butt as if I held it firm in my hand, such is the sure remembrance of a sense of touch—like the muttered oaths and fierce shouts of Lachlann Ban, had been part of a sleep drugged nightmare.

"Here, take this, and be quick about it."

The voice came from below. I pushed the blankets aside, and got to my knees, still heavy with sleep. It was Lachlann Ban, reaching up with a mug of steaming hot tea and a huge circle of girdle scone. The scone was spread thick with crowdie. I squatted cross-legged in the hay, wolfing the scone and crowdie, and taking quick sips at the tea. The tea was good, strong and sweet and scalding hot, but it stung my cut lips something terrible.

"I never heard you get up," I said, peering down at him and trying to blink the sleep out of my eyes. "You should ha' wakened me, Lachlann."

All I was seeing was the top of his head, his straw-coloured thatch curling thick about his ears. But at my words he put his head back and looked up, and I am telling you there was no sleep in those flinty blue eyes of his, and precious little pleasure at the sight of me so far as I could see.

"What do you think I have been at this while back," he demanded, "but trying to get you to stir? As well for me to try to raise the dead as rouse you, boy. A man would be needing to sound trumpets—and close to your ear at that— to have a hope o' waking you swift."

At home, the *cailleach* and Mairi were always on at me for being slow in rising, and I took not the least heed of their nagging, regarding it as the right of womenfolk to make a noise seeing they were always first up, and bound to be jealous of the menfolk who were not charged with the duty of getting the house on the go. But it was different when Lachlann Ban started on the same tack, and I was wild with myself for having slept so sound. It was that dim in the byre there was no knowing the time of day by the light, and I was almost afraid to ask.

"What time is it?" I said, shamefaced.

"Past midday," he said, "and there is something queer on the go or I swear this place has changed something terrible since I was away. We had best make for the sheepcote where we can get a sight o' the whole township."

I pulled on my boots and slid down the hay to the floor. Lachlann Ban unbolted the door at the gable end of the byre. "Keep right at my back," he said, "and do as I do."

The house and byre nestled in a hollow out of sight of the rest of the township. At the byre end of the house there was a thick cluster of rowan trees, arching round to the hill at the back. On the other side of the rowans the ground rose steeply in a rocky knoll. Perched on the knoll, seeming as much a part of the natural growth as the rowans, was the sheepcote; a tiny building of low drystone walls and roof thatched with rushes, like a proper house in miniature.

Lachlann Ban crouched close to the ground and ran for the trees. I was right at his back. He bounded up the knoll, flattened himself against the wet rocks, and peered cautiously over the top. A short run and the two of us were crouched against the side wall of the sheepcote. Lachlann Ban went down on his belly and put his head around the corner, masked by the ferns that grew thick. He drew back, and said, "Inside, as fast as you can." Bent double, we shot around the corner of the sheepcote and plunged through the open door. He closed the door, and squatted down on his heels among the dry sheep droppings on the earthen floor. "Take a good look about," he said, "and tell me what you see."

The door was made of driftwood, rough boards with many a gap between. I had a clear enough view of our township all the way from the circling hills in the west to the river and the road north beyond the bridge to the inn and the lodge. I could see the whole sweep of the bay, the breakers flushing the shore, and the crofts of the next township stretching green to the sea.

It was raining, a fine steady drizzle, the mist clinging low to the hills, the air that still every house in sight carried a heavy plume of blue smoke anchored fast to the thatch— all except the manse and Seamus Sionnach's white house where the smoke rose slow from stone chimneys. Down on Seamus Sionnach's croft his wife and two sons were busy lifting potatoes. There was not another living soul to be seen.

Three times I scoured the land in search of another human form, straining my eyes along the length of the road, crossing every croft in turn, lingering about the doors of byres and houses. The place was deserted. There was no one to be seen. I looked down at Lachlann Ban, squatting silent in the dark sheepcote, not knowing what to say to him.

"Take a look through the peephole there," he said, pointing to a narrow slit in the wall on the right. "That will give you a sight o' the smithy and the crofts on that side."

I put my eye to the slit, that slow on the uptake I was looking for a trail of smoke above Colla's smithy, although my ears should have told me the forge would be cold and dead as there had been no clatter of hammer on anvil, and it the very day when sound would carry sharp and clear. The door of the smithy was shut, no crowd about it either, and the smithy the one place where they all gathered to pass the time of day. And even supposing there was too much work on the go for the most of them to idle in talk, never a day passed without the old men being clustered thick about the smithy eager for news.

My eyes searched Coinneach the Piper's croft; quartered the crofts of Iain Beag, Tomas the Elder—and he was a demon for work, the last man to let a potato lie in the ground because there was a spit of rain in the air—Eachunn Ruadh, Fearghus Mor, Old Diarmad. All deserted. Not a one of them to be seen, nor any of their kin.

I turned to Lachlann Ban, my head bent against the low roof. "It is queer, right enough," I said, wondering what was doing at home, because I could not see our own croft for a rise in the ground. "Seamus Sionnach's crowd are the only ones working at potatoes, and there are plenty wi' tatties still to be lifted. I never saw the township so quiet, except when there was a death in the place, and even then you would see someone moving on the road or putting out a beast or even just standing about sniffing the air."

"Aye, but the *cailleach* would have had word if there had been a death in the place, and no one has come near her," Lachlann Ban said. "And you may be sure the plague did not strike in the night. So where are they?"

"Inside, about the fire."

"And what man in this place would not be for making out once he was into his boots and the day half decent?"

"Every one o' them," I said, "unless they were ashamed to show face."

"*Dhia*, boy!" he cried, "I believe you have it. Maybe they got word."

"Word?"

"Word o' the eviction."

"But how? Seamus Sionnach is not the one to let on."

"No, not him. But how does word ever get about in this place? I am telling you we are not needing the telegraph so long as the lairds and the factors and the tacksmen and the lawyers have servants. They forget their servants have ears—and the Gaelic. And the word is passed on in the Gaelic, quick as the wind." He brought his fist down into his palm, and sprang to his feet, cracking his head on a roof beam. He joined me at the door, peering through a gap in the boards. "That will be it, right enough. They will have got word o' the eviction, and they are ashamed to show face."

"Aye, and afraid," I said. "They know fine they will not be spared now that Major Traill is back. They will be busy counting the pennies for the rent collection on Monday."

Lachlann Ban let rip an oath; a long, terrible oath in the Gaelic that would not be the same at all supposing I tried to put it into English. And then he cried, "I see them!"

He was the longest-sighted man I ever knew, able to spot his sheep on a gathering day at a distance that was beyond the rest of us, so I did not waste time looking. I asked him what he had seen.

"A wagonette," he said, "coming on to the bend above

the inn. That will be the sheriff officer's party, and all for one widow woman. I wonder what like a crowd they would have supposing it was a man wi' grown sons they were after evicting."

The wagonette was round the bend and on to the straight leading to the bridge before I spotted it. We watched in silence as it drew off the road by the mill. Three men climbed out. They were joined by a fourth who had been waiting under the trees by the mill.

"Seamus Sionnach," Lachlann Ban said, and spat. "The ground officer is wanting in at the kill."

"Lachlann," I said in wonder, afraid my eyes were deceiving me, "do you see them? Over by Somhairle's house— and Martainn's and Colla's. There are *cailleachs* on the move."

"I see them," he said.

He crossed swiftly to the slit in the wall, and whistled softly between his teeth. I was at his back, and he drew aside to let me see. There were old *cailleachs*, near a score of them, all making for the path that led past the smithy to Lachlann Ban's croft. I saw the grandmother of Iain Beag among them, old Seonag, hirpling along on her stick, herself near ninety if she was a day, with a tongue on her that would put fear into the hearts of the brave.

We went back to the door. Seamus Sionnach and the three men from the wagonette were marching in line up the road from the bridge. They passed the school, and I lost sight of them where the rising ground hid the start of the track to the smithy.

The *cailleachs* were the first to come into view, hurrying past the silent smithy, a flooding tide of black on the brown of the track—black bonnets, black shawls, black skirts, black boots—and I must say the very sight of them put a queer tingle of fear down my spine, foolish as that may seem. They formed up in a black line not a score of paces from the door of the sheepcote, where the path dipped down to the house. And they stood with their backs to the house, old Seonag in the centre of the line, in advance of the others.

The four men came into view near the smithy, walking two abreast, Seamus Sionnach clacking away with a red-faced man who carried a stick, the other two shambling along behind.

"The red-faced fellow is MacDonald, the sheriff officer," Lachlann Ban whispered.

"Who are the other two?"

"Helpers. Any rag in need of a shilling or two and a dram at the end o' the day. No decent man would be seen dead at this kind o' work."

As they came near the line of *cailleachs*, the sheriff officer and Seamus Sionnach stopped. They had to, unless they were to force a way through.

"I must ask you to step aside, ladies," the sheriff officer said, "and let me proceed with my business." He had the Gaelic, too, for a wonder.

"Business?" It was old Seonag who spoke, and you would never know she was near ninety, the voice on her was that strong. "What honest business would the like o' this beauty be on?" She prodded the biggest of the two men in the rear with her stick, a dark fellow with no brow on him, whose bushy eyebrows very near met his hair. "I mind that face. He has the look of a Fraser to me."

"Aye, Tomas Fraser it is," the sheriff officer said, as cheery as you please. "You have a sharp eye, Mistress MacLeod. His father was a drover dealing in these parts, but that was all o' thirty years ago."

"Some drover," old Seonag cackled. "I mind him well.

The same one had to flee the place wi' the name o' sheep stealer on him. But bad an' all as the father was I doubt the son is worse. Good grief, the sheep must be thin on the ground if a Fraser has to earn his bread by putting poor widow women from their own hearth."

"I have my duty to do, Mistress MacLeod," the sheriff officer said, "and I must ask you to step aside or it will be the worse for your son and the sons of the rest of you here."

"It is not my son who is here," old Seonag spat at him, "nor my grandson even. It is me." She took a step forward, her right hand clutching her stick, her left hand thrust out like a claw. "And I am telling you, MacDonald, I will call on God to curse you through ten generations and all eternity supposing you put the Widow MacGregor from her door."

"Aye, curses on you," the *cailleachs* hissed.

The sheriff officer stood his ground, but his red face had paled, and little wonder. Old Seonag's hair had come loose, and was hanging free down her back, and what with her long white hair hanging wild, and the way she was bent forward over her stick, she had the look of a right witch. Tomas Fraser, the son of the sheep stealer, and the other rag along with him—a thin-faced fellow, who was for ever plucking nervously at his long nose—had drawn back. Indeed, I believe the pair of them would have made off there and then if Seamus Sionnach had not seized Seonag roughly by the arm, and cried, "Are you wise, woman? If it was not for me taking your part wi' the factor, the whole crowd o' you that is behind wi' the rent would be cleared from the place this day. Away to your fire, and let men be about their business." He pushed her aside and strode on down to the house, the other three hard on his heels. Old

Seonag drew her shawl about her and followed them, the other *cailleachs* close at her back.

The sheriff officer hammered on the door with his stick. Lachlann Ban's mother was not slow in opening, and she flung the door wide. She was carrying a stick herself, and she faced him squarely.

"Widow MacGregor," he said, holding out a paper to her, "I have to serve you with notice to——"

She tried to strike the paper out of his hand with her stick, but he was too quick for her, stepping back swiftly. "Away wi' your papers," she cried, and there was a shrill chorus of assent from the *cailleachs*. "I am not for moving supposing there were a dozen like you at my door."

Safe out of striking distance of the widow's stick, the sheriff officer beckoned to Fraser. As the son of the sheep stealer stepped forward, Lachlann Ban's mother let fly. Well, I am telling you, if that blow had caught him on the head she would have felled him for sure, but he ducked at the last moment. The stick came down on his back with a *thwack* that must have been heard in Garos across the moor, and snapped in two. Fraser seized her by the wrist, and the thin-faced fellow was quick to fasten on her other arm. The two of them dragged her away from the door.

"Lachlann!" she cried. "Lachlann!"

"You will need to shout louder, Mistress MacGregor," Seamus Sionnach sneered, "if your voice is to carry the length o' America."

As the ground officer started to speak, Lachlann Ban pushed me aside and flung open the door of the sheepcote. No hawk ever fell on his prey with a swifter strike. The words were hardly off Seamus Sionnach's lips when he was seized from behind and flung to the ground. His bonnet fell off, showing his great dome of a head, bald as an egg and cleft with the terrible scar. One of the *cailleachs*—the mother of Coinneach the Piper, and herself well up in years—scooped up a big pat of cow dung and dropped it on his head, as neat as you please.

Tomas Fraser let go of the widow's wrist, but before he could get his fist up Lachlann Ban had hit him—once, twice, thrice—and that was the son of the sheep stealer flat on his back. The *cailleach* picked up the top half of her broken stick and brought it down on the head of the thin-faced fellow. He took two faltering steps forward and three shaky ones back. Widow MacGregor hit him a ringing slap across the face with the flat of her hand, and he toppled over the feet of his partner and joined him on the ground.

The sheriff officer turned from pinning a paper to the door. Lachlann Ban seized him by the throat. MacDonald's face was not red now; it had paled to a sickly grey. "*Dhia*, Lachlann," he gasped, "they told me you were in America."

"Did they now?" Lachlann Ban's voice was that soft I had to strain my ears to catch the words. "That was fine for you, eh?—me in America, and yourself here fine and handy for putting my mother from the croft."

"Not me," he said. "Not me, Lachlann. The law just. It is there, writ plain, on the notice I was to serve."

"The law?" Lachlann Ban was roaring now, his voice beating like a flail about the ears of the hapless sheriff officer. "Was it the law that worked this land before me and my father? Was it the law that cleared the rocks and raised the dykes and dug the drains and drove back the heather and the rushes? Was it the law that put sweat into the land and laboured strong to keep it in good heart? Or was it my father's father, and his father before him? Aye, and generations o' MacGregors beyond number, themselves the keepers o' the land long before there was word o' the English law in this place. You think they toiled for this—for me and the *cailleach* to be cleared from the land by a piece o' paper?" He shifted his grip to the front of the sheriff officer's coat, and lifted him clean off his feet, and shook him as if he was of no more substance than a half-empty bag of meal, and set him down again. "Do not talk to me of the law, MacDonald. The law is the word o' that rag of a factor."

"You know me, Lachlann," the sheriff officer protested. "I am not for making trouble. I have my job to do just. A man must do his job or his family would perish."

"I will give you a job to do, MacDonald," Lachlann Ban said. "You can burn the summons you brought here."

"Aye, surely," the sheriff officer said, craven now that his helpers had been beaten to their knees, and Seamus Sionnach had slunk off, dripping dung. "Whatever you say, Lachlann."

"Away and fetch a lighted peat," Lachlann Ban told his mother.

When she went into the house I cast a quick look round. Lachlann Ban had talked about word spreading quick in this place. He did not know how true he spoke. Some of the old *cailleachs* had hurried away the moment he rushed out of the sheepcote. Old and halt they may have been, but they were not slow in spreading the word. The news of his return must have roared through the township like a heather fire fanned by an easterly gale. I never saw the like. The place was black with people, men running from all quarters, old and young, the supple and the lame, every one of them striding out as fast as he could go, and all of them converging on Lachlann Ban's croft, as if the Gates of the Kingdom had opened wide there, bidding them enter.

I ran down the path to join him, and it was as well that

I did. By the time the widow had emerged with a glowing peat, close on two score men were gathered in a ring around the sheriff officer and his helpers.

The sheriff officer held the paper out to the glowing peat, but it was too damp to catch alight. "Blow on the peat," Lachlann Ban commanded. The sheriff officer did as he was bid. The bright peat burst into flame, and he held it obediently on high, so that all could see, and put the paper to the flame. As it burned away, a great cheer burst from the swelling crowd.

If Lachlann Ban was pleased you would never know by the look on his face. "Down on your knees, MacDonald," he said.

The sheriff officer licked his lips, his eyes flickering around the growing throng about him. He got down awkwardly on his knees in the wet grass.

"Say after me—As I am before God."

"*As I am before God.*"

"I will never serve another notice of eviction."

"*I will never serve another notice . . .*"

"Of eviction."

"*Of eviction.*"

"On any man."

"*On any man.*"

"Or woman."

"*Or woman.*"

"In this place."

"*In this place.*"

"I give my oath."

"*I give my oath.*"

"Before God."

"*Before God.*"

There was a silence, not a sound to be heard but the sudden, sharp intake of breath, as if everyone there had forgotten to breathe during the taking of the oath. The sheriff officer got to his feet, wiping the sweat from his face.

Lachlann Ban lifted his hands high, and cried out to all those assembled there, "Make way for Sheriff Officer MacDonald and his men. We will see them clear o' the township boundary."

The crowd parted, and the sheriff officer and his helpers started forward. They were lonely men, I am telling you, because Lachlann Ban gave them a good ten yards' start, as if they were unclean, and it was wise to keep your distance from them.

That was the way we moved off: Three men out in front—the sheriff officer in the lead, his helpers at his heels like beaten curs—then a gap, and then a great procession, more than a hundred strong, close-knit, marching shoulder to shoulder.

As the three in front drew level with the smithy, the mother of Colla the smith rushed out and flung a pail of slops over the sheriff officer's helpers. But it was when we reached the school that the fun started.

The scholars must have got word of the ongoings, and they were breaking out of school. The *Maighstir* stood at the door, the two women teachers on either side of him, the three of them with arms spread wide trying to stem the rush to the gates. One of the teachers went down, and the scholars broke clear, pouring out to the gates. The *Maighstir* turned and chased a red-haired fellow, the younger brother of Eachunn Ruadh, across the yard. He seized the boy by his ragged coat as he tried to climb the wall. There was the sound of ripping cloth; the young fellow was over the wall, and the *Maighstir* down on his backside, clutching a piece of coat in his hands.

The scholars danced around the three in front, jeering and hooting. As we neared the bridge, a cry went up, "In the river wi' them! Throw them in the river!"

There was a crowd from the next township gathered at the far end of the bridge. An angry growl went up from them at the sight of the sheriff officer and his men. The three of them stopped, afraid to go forward, and unable to turn back. The sight of the waiting wagonette outside the mill was too much for Tomas Fraser. He leapt on to the parapet of the bridge and started to run.

It all happened so quickly I could not say in truth how it came about. There were stones flying right enough, but whether he was hit or lost his footing on the wet parapet, I do not know. One moment he was running along the narrow parapet, and the next he was clawing at air as he plummeted down into the rock-strewn river. He was swept under the arch of the bridge, and vanished downstream where the willows hung low over the deep pool.

Lachlann Ban stripped off his coat and raced down the bank. He plunged in to the swift-flowing river, striking out for the pool. I ran down the steep bank, and clutched at the stem of a willow. I watched him dive into the dark pool. Twice he came up for air, and the third time he had Tomas Fraser by the collar. Willing hands seized the two of them and hauled them out of the water. Blood was oozing from a great gash in the head of Tomas Fraser. When they carried him up the bank, water spouted from his mouth.

A strong hand gripped my arm and pulled me round. It was my father. "Good grief, boy, what have you been up to?" He was that excited he could hardly get the words out. "They say the police have a warrant for your arrest, and Uilleam Mor has named you for a horse thief." He stared at me as if he beheld a stranger before him. "Your mother is near out o' her mind."

The hubbub of voices about us was suddenly still. Lachlann Ban laid a hand on my father's shoulder. The pair of us turned to face him. His dripping hair was plastered wetly about his face, and his sodden clothes clung tight to his body. He brushed the wet from his eyes, and looked down at Tomas Fraser, stretched flat on the bank.

The son of the sheep stealer never moved. The blood from the wound in his head was a dark smear across the white of his cheek. A frond of green stuff was caught up in his tangled hair.

"The police will be hunting more than Alasdair once the factor and his friends get busy," Lachlann Ban said. He bent down and removed the green stuff. "This fellow is dead, and they will be fine pleased to call it murder."

10

The body of Tomas Fraser was put aboard the wagonette, wrapped in a length of sailcloth and laid on neatly spread meal sacks borrowed from the mill. Storm clouds were gathering fast about the hills; one black monster of a cloud hung low over the pass in the Quiraing, coiling across the green of the foothills. A flash of sheet lightning lit the sky above Beinn Edra, and a long, slow rumble of thunder echoed about the hills. The rain came lashing down, whipped on by a freshening breeze of wind out of the west.

The crowd had diminished by the time the wagonette moved off, but it was not the heavy rain that sent them scurrying for home; they were too well acquaint with wet weather to seek shelter at the start of a downpour. It was fear that had them moving. I knew fine that among the first to slink away were the very ones who had been shouting the loudest to throw the three of them in the river. You can always tell the craven by the noise they make when they think they have the upper hand.

Those of us who were left watched in silence as the driver urged his horses forward, and the wagonette jolted on to the road and picked up speed. The sheriff officer kept glancing back over his shoulder, as if unable to believe that they would be allowed to make off unmolested. It was the custom with us to pay a decent respect to the dead, but the sheriff officer was made bold by our silence. He got to his feet, and cupped his hands to his mouth, and shouted, "You will pay dear for this day's work, MacGregor."

Eachunn Ruadh's younger brother, Aonghas, snatched up a stone, but before he could hurl it after the retreating wagonette, Lachlann Ban gripped his wrist. "Time enough for stones when they are seeking us out," he said. "Put your backside to them, boy, and let MacDonald's words beat on empty air."

As Aonghas let go of the stone, Lachlann Ban laid an arm about the boy's thin shoulders. He swung him round, and started off back across the bridge. I heard him say, "We will be glad enough of your help before we are done, Aonghas, you may be sure o' that."

He was a great hand at making folk feel important, Lachlann Ban, and there was never the least difference in his manner supposing he was speaking to a twelve-year-old like Aonghas, or a man well up in years, the like of Old Diarmad, who was past the eighty mark. No matter who you were, or how poor an opinion others might have of you, he had the knack of making you feel you were important to *him*. I suppose that was why there were so many of us ready to come running the moment he gave us the nod. Aonghas—who was never out of trouble in the school, and was for ever getting the belt from the *Maighstir* for speaking out of turn—would have sat mute at his feet for a twelve-month, obedient as the born slave of a Turkish pasha, if Lachlann Ban had so desired.

Mind you, I knew of one who could not abide Lachlann, and that was my own mother. And I was in dread when we reached the track that wound round the back of the school to our croft, seeing my father was dead keen to haul him straight home with us. I knew fine there would be a big enough racket from the *cailleach* when I showed face, and if I was to walk in alongside Lachlann Ban that would be her up to high doh, and no knowing what she might say or do. I could just see her screeching at him that he was to blame for everything that had happened to me, and the thought of the way she might shame me turned me sick in the stomach.

But Lachlann Ban resisted all the *bodach's* entreaties, saying he must change into dry gear, and make preparations for off. "Away you go," he said, "and see that Alasdair gets a good bite o' food in him. The police will be hunting the pair of us before another day is past, and I am not for making it easy for them. Alasdair and me will need to take to the heather before this night is done, and the sooner we are clear o' the township the better."

"Aye, but the rent collection is on Monday," my father said. "What are we to do, Lachlann? The most o' them will listen to you, and right enough I believe they will stand fast this time. But without you they will troop to the Lodge as quiet as sheep, and hand over their last penny, supposing that is them starving for the rest o' the winter."

"I am not for fleeing the place," Lachlann Ban said, in that calm, unhurried way of his, as if he alone had the course plotted clear and had taken stock of the hidden reefs that startled other men by their sudden appearance. "I am just not for staying quiet by the fire so that all the police need do is march in the door and clap chains on me. And I am not for seeing this fellow"—he jerked a thumb at me—"flung in the jail at the notion of Uilleam Mor. Away home now." His eyes met mine briefly, and I wondered how much he perceived of the relief I felt within me. "I will be over later wi' Eachunn and Iain and the rest o' them, and I will tell you then what I have in mind for the day o' the rent collection."

I was ready for the *cailleach* the moment we stepped inside the door, but I am telling you I got some shock at the sight of her. It was too dark in the kitchen to make out the faces of Mairi and Seoras, but I knew fine by the way they were sitting quiet on the bench that there was trouble on the go. One look at my mother's face and it was easy seen why there was not a cheep out of either of them.

She was crouched low on her birch-bough stool by the fire, sunk that deep in a brooding melancholy it was no wonder that Mairi and Seoras did not have a word to utter. Her face was half in shadow, half lit by the leaping peat fire flames, but I could see enough of her to know what to expect. Her long hair, which she always wore coiled in a bun at the nape of her neck, hung untended down her back, as if she had newly risen from her bed. She had the same deep-sunken, darkly shadowed eyes as her father, the old *Ceistear*, but now they were that underscored with black, the skin looked bruised, and her eyelids were puffed and swollen, red with weeping.

But it was not just her face that mirrored the change in her; it was her body, too. The way her back was bowed— and not just from crouching on a low stool. The way her shoulders drooped. The way her hands hung limply in her lap—and herself the one whose hands were never idle from morn to night—all made up the picture of a person who had been crushed by a burden too heavy to bear. She had aged something terrible, the *cailleach*, and it not three days since I had last seen her.

She lifted her head slowly, hearing the door open, and her dull eyes surveyed my father without interest. But when she saw me at his back there was a sharpening in her look, the slackness about her face was gone, the features drawn together all of a sudden into a purposeful whole. She rose from her stool, and came at me with slow, slow steps, for all the world like a sleepwalker on the prowl. I thought she was going to strike me, and I stepped back quickly. I stumbled over Mairi's legs, and sat down heavily on the bench.

But she never lifted a finger. Her hands stayed tight clasped at her breast, kneading together as if she was working at dough. "Well, you are back," she said, her voice flat, dry as her lank hair, "and not lacking in brass neck seeing you have the face to walk in as calm as you please and take your ease on the bench as if that was your rightful due. You flaunt your shame like a tinker, boy. I am telling you, that worldly pride o' yours will be your undoing. And what am I to tell the *Maighstir*, and himself fair distracted since he was the one to give you your chance? Am I to tell him you fled the inn after two days, like a thief in the night, and not content wi' running from your master made havoc o' the good man's cellar?"

"Your father would ha' sounded a glad amen to that," the *bodach* chipped in. "Many's the jug o' good whisky he smashed in his day."

That was a right stinger, but our father could have been on the far side of Beinn Edra for all the heed she paid him. I doubt if she heard a single word. Her whole being was taken up with me. She would have been deaf to the tumult of a multitude at that moment.

"You are far gone in wrongdoing, I am telling you, boy," she swept on, "when your master is after setting the police on you, and naming you for a horse thief. Good grief, it is as well for us all that *my* father is not here to witness the shame you have brought on this house, and himself never near the police, nor a wrong deed ever held to his name—no, not in all the days of his life. It is a blessing just he was taken before you were right set in your wicked ways."

"Be quiet, woman," my father said. "Mairi, light the lamp."

"Quiet?" she screeched. "Me? I have been quiet too long and that is the truth of it. Who are you calling on me to be quiet and your own cousin busy bringing shame on our name, himself lying in the jail in Portree charged wi' mobbing and rioting? And this one certain sure to land up in the jail along wi' him from all I hear. It is a wonder to me there is grey in your beard, man. You speak that foolish at times a person could believe you were not long out o' the school."

"Be quiet, woman," my father thundered; aye *thundered*— and I saw him as he must have been before there was grey in his beard, and the bleak years had taken their grim toll; saw him as he was before the Russian shot destroyed his good right arm, and he was strong and unafraid and his own master, when he would have laughed at the notion that one day he might have to call for aid to tie his boots.

He strode to the table and snatched up the lamp that Mairi had lit, and held it so that the light shone on my face. "See the boy's face?" he said to the *cailleach*. "Look well upon it, woman. That was the work of your holy friend, Uilleam Mor, him who helped build the new kirk out o' the wealth he plundered from the people." He thrust the lamp into her hand, and pulled down the neck of my jersey. "See the marks on him?—near strangled he was by Uilleam Mor. And for why? Because the same fine gentleman could not wait to hear it was not Alasdair who created the havoc you speak of. As for my cousin, Tormod, you know fine there is not a quieter man in the place. They call him Parnell half in joke just, because he cannot speak to a person without sounding like he was laying off to a meeting—and a big one at that. Mobbing and rioting? Parnell? The same one was trying to quieten the crowd at Valtos when the police arrested him. Well, wait you," he said, seeing the disbelief stamped plain on her face, "there is a Mr. Drummond in Portree, a lawyer come all the way from Inverness to defend him, and I am telling you Mr. Drummond is the very one to have Parnell out o' the jail and a free man in the morning."

She put down the lamp on the table, and gave one of her sniffs at me, and said, "Well, then, your lawyer man can get this boy out o' the trouble he is in."

"Have sense, woman," my father protested. "Tormod has witnesses galore ready to swear he never lifted a finger, and was busy telling the folk to go quiet to their homes when the police laid hands on him. But where are the witnesses for Alasdair? If it is to be his word against the like of Uilleam Mor and the factor, a whole coach load o' lawyers would never keep him clear o' the jail."

"If he has done no wrong," she said, stubborn as ever, "the Lord will protect him."

"Well, we will see about that." The *bodach* sat down on the bench beside me. "Get a bite o' hot food prepared for Alasdair," he added, in a gentler tone. "Mairi, away and give your mother a hand. The boy cannot bide under a roof to-night for fear the police raid the place. He will need a right good feed before he makes off. There is no knowing when they will get their next bite. Lachlann Ban is handy enough, but when a man takes to the heather he cannot be giving his stomach justice at all, at all."

The *cailleach* paused in the act of hanging the heavy broth pot on its iron hook above the fire. "Lachlann Ban?" she said.

"Aye, the shouts we heard were right enough," my father went on, giving me a warning prod with his knee. "Lachlann Ban is back, and seeing he humbled the sheriff officer and put him clear o' the township, himself and Alasdair are in the same boat."

I realised then that the *cailleach* had not heard of the dead man in the river. She must have barred the door on Mairi and Seoras when the word spread that Lachlann Ban was back and our father made off. No wonder Mairi had a lip on her you could near have sat on. But even without the knowledge that Lachlann Ban would be blamed for the death that had taken place—and she would have been one of the first to cry murder—she was not pleased to hear his name linked with mine. As she hung the pot on the hook, she could not hold back the flooding tears from her eyes, and when she called on Seoras to fetch fresh peats there was a sob in her voice. But she never said another word, and once I was fed—and by that time Tomas the Elder and half a dozen others had crowded in—she made off quietly to her bed.

Lachlann Ban came in with Iain Beag and Eachunn Ruadh and Coinneach the Piper and Colla the smith close at his heels, and half a score more jostling hard at their back. He was carrying a canvas bag over his shoulder, and he pushed it under the bench. At the sight of him, there was an excited babel of voices, near every man in the room— and some of those standing outside, crammed about the open door—besieging him with questions. The *bodach* nudged me, and whispered, "You had best have a word wi' your mother before you make off. She has taken this bad, mind."

There was a *cruisgean* burning on the chest by her bed. The movement of the door started the smoky flame on a mad dance, but the *cailleach* never stirred. She was lying on her back, the blankets drawn up to her chin, her eyes tight shut.

Colla the smith's great rumbling roar of a laugh rang out, and the voices in the kitchen, strange as it may seem, sounded louder than when I had been among them on the other side of the driftwood partition. It seemed as if there was never less than a score of tongues on the go at the same time such was the clamour they made, the words fairly bubbling from their lips they had that much to put tongue to—and me standing there at the bedside of my mother struck dumb, that nervous I could not keep from tracing patterns on the hard packed earthen floor with the toe of my boot, as if I was back in the school and waiting on a belting from the *Maighstir*.

"Is your head paining you?" I managed at last.

"Ach, I am weary, boy," she said, "weary just." Her eyes stayed shut.

I looked down at her, not knowing what to say, trying to follow the confused babel of voices in the kitchen, desperate eager—if the truth be told—to be back among them, and ashamed, at the same time, that I should want to be gone from her, and barely a word spoken. I struggled to find something to say, but my tongue had gone dead on me, and I could not have uttered a word supposing she had placed a gold sovereign in my hand.

"You will be wanting off," she said, and I was possessed of a sudden dread that she could read my thoughts. "You had best away."

"Ach, time enough," I said. "Lachlann Ban is not long here, and they all have plenty to say to him."

I could have bitten off my tongue the moment I spoke, but all she said was, "Aye, they will have plenty to say."

"Well, he has been away a long time." I stopped, conscious I was treading dangerous ground, but too confused to change course. I stumbled on, sinking deeper into the bog. "They got a surprise," I said, "seeing he came back so sudden."

She pushed herself up on one arm, and her eyes were open now and on my face. Seeing she was weeping, I stared down at my boots. "Why could he not have perished," she said fiercely, "like many a one who set out from these parts for America? Why did he have to come back to plague us? But he has come, and you are off with him. Well, if you are going, go. You had best be gone before Seoras is old enough to take the fever from you. I have no mind to see little Seoras treading the same restless road. It took the loss of an arm to quieten your father, but I doubt you will never cease from strife this side o' the grave."

"*Dhia*, I am not away for good," I cried.

"Do not take the name o' the Lord in vain, or His wrath will strike you like the forked tongues of serpents."

I looked at her. She had her eyes tight shut again, her hands clasped under her chin. I wondered if she was praying.

"Well, I had best be off," I said.

She was silent, only a twitching of her lips showing she was not sleeping. "I am sorry about the trouble at the inn," I said, "and you can tell the *Maighstir* it was not me did the damage, but if he knew what like a man Uilleam Mor is he would not be grieving for him."

"I am not wanting to hear," she said.

"Well, then, I had best away."

I opened the door, and the flame of the *cruisgean* flickered and went out. The stink of the smoking wick was strong in the room. "Are you wanting the lamp lit?" I said. She did not speak. I waited, but there was still no word from her, so I shut the door behind me, and went back to the crowded kitchen.

Lachlann Ban was saying, "No, no, Tomas, you have got it wrong."

Tomas the Elder snatched off his bonnet and scrubbed at his bald head with the flat of his hand. He clapped on his bonnet again, and said, "I am not so sure. A man is dead, and a helper o' the law at that. A helper o' the law, mind."

"A Judas!" Colla the smith roared. "Who but a Judas would carry out the like o' that work, and all for a handful o' pennies?"

"No matter," Tomas persisted, "that is not the way they will be looking at it away from here. Many's the time the marines have been brought in for less. And if they bring in the marines there will be no word of a rent collection on Monday. They will tear the roofs from our houses and clear the lot of us from the place."

"No, Tomas, you are wrong," Lachlann Ban said evenly. "It is me they will be after, and I will see to it that they are kept busy on the hunt. Alasdair will be along wi' me, and Iain Beag and Eachunn Ruadh are for joining us, too. So you may be sure the sins o' this place will be set square on the heads o' the four of us, once they find we are gone."

My father's voice rose above the stormy clatter of tongues. "So we go meek to the slaughter at the rent collection on Monday, is that the way of it? We pay what we have, and near every man in the place beggared the long winter

130

through, not a penny for food or medicines or gear or the like, and no hope o' raising a shilling until the coming o' the spring sales when we can sell a beast or two. Is that to be the way of it?"

Lachlann Ban raised his hands high, quelling the noisy babble of talk. "I want every one o' you to show face at the rent collection." He lifted his hands again, silencing the rumble of dissent. "Every one o' you, mind. The clerk will ask you for the rent, and tell the amount of arrears you are owing."

"Fine we know that, Lachlann," Tomas the Elder growled. "It is finding the money that would baffle a body."

"Aye, but he will ask you more," Lachlann Ban went on evenly. "He will ask you what money you have managed to raise for the rent, and what you are left with in the house, and how much you are owing at the shop. And if there is a man among you wi' cash enough for the rent and more besides to see him through the winter"—here there were cries of, "Seamus Sionnach, who else!"—"that man will pay his rent. But those who would be left without a penny will be told they can hold back the rent. All I am asking of you is that each one o' you speak out true on the day o' the collection."

There was a long, stunned silence, broken by a mad clamour of voices.

"Away, Lachlann!"

"You are after having us on, man!"

"The water in the spring will turn to whisky, Lachlann, before the factor will let us hold back the rent."

"You think he is worrying because we are owing at the shop?"

"The same one is not caring supposing there is famine in the place, and we are bleeding the cattle for food."

"What way can you know the questions they will put to us at the rent collection?"

"I know fine the question they will be asking—where is the rent money?"

"Aye, and a man must pay up—supposing that is his last penny gone—or lose the right of a roof for his family."

"Right enough, they would like fine to clear us out and make the whole township into one big tack. That was the way of it at Glenuig, the crofters cleared, and Uilleam Mor made king."

"No, no, Lachlann says the factor will see us right."

"Aye, fine we know Major Traill, and him that generous he would strip the shirt from his back and hand it to the first one he saw in need!"

"I am telling you, Lachlann, there will be vineyards sprouting on the bare rock o' Beinn Edra before that rag of a factor has a change o' heart."

The voices swirled and clashed about him, but he remained unmoved, repeating calmly, "Do as I say. Do as I say. I give you——" He stopped suddenly, swinging round to face the door. We had all heard the shrill shout outside, and every man's tongue was stilled. After the hubbub of noise, the sudden silence struck chill as an empty cavern in the hill where the least sound lingers long—and, my word, the thin note of that shrill shout stayed fast in the ear of everyone there. You could see that by the way they all froze, heads cocked, anxious eyes fixed on the door.

Those at the door flattened back. A small, thin figure bored through the throng to Lachlann Ban's side. He was swaying on his feet, panting like a spent dog, his eyes—and he had always had bulging eyes, Aonghas, giving him a look of startled wonder, like a wild creature strange to the haunts of men—near popping from his head.

"Quick, Lachlann!" he gasped, his lungs that greedy for air he could hardly mouth the words. "The police are come!" He tugged at Lachlann Ban's arm, as if to jerk him into action. "The place is swarming wi' them!"

II

A whistle shrilled, loud and clear. It seemed to come from the direction of the school, but it was hard to tell from within the house with its drystone walls near the width of the span of a man's arms. Two short blasts sounded, as if in answer, and I could have sworn they were blown from the other side of us, above the township gate.

Iain Beag started for the door. "There is a ring o' lanterns hard about us," Aonghas cried. "And they are searching the houses. I saw three o' them making for Coinneach's door."

Coinneach's croft was next to the school. Our township was cleft in two by the road and the river. There were six crofts in the south-east corner above the school, starting with Coinneach the Piper's and ending with the croft of Old Diarmad, whose outer boundaries came up against the drystone wall marking the start of the rough grazing. Our own croft marched with Diarmad's.

"Make up the back behind the stackyard, Iain," Lachlann Ban said calmly. "Eachunn, go with him. Try to make a count o' the lanterns."

As they shot out of the door, he turned to the rest of them. "Make for home," he commanded. "The womenfolk will be needing you if there are police bursting in on them. And if they ha' ringed us, it will keep them busy sorting you all out, and give us time before they are at the door."

134

They streamed out of the kitchen, jostling in the doorway they were that eager to be gone; all but Aonghas, who remained rooted fast to Lachlann Ban's side. "You did well, boy," my father said, "but you had best make off wi' the rest or they will be worrying at home."

He shook his head. "I am for staying along wi' Lachlann."

"Aye, and welcome," Lachlann Ban said, and to hear him speak you would have taken Aonghas to be the size of Colla the smith, not a boy of twelve, with shoulders on him as narrow as a girl's, "but I have other work for you, Aonghas, and it is sleep you are needing to-night if you are to tackle it. Make over to Alasdair Rob to-morrow"—he nodded at my father, an unspoken message passing between them as their eyes met—"and he will tell you what I want doing. I am depending on you, mind."

"Aye, surely, Lachlann," Aonghas said, and he went off with a step on him as proud as Coinneach at the head of a procession when his pipes are sounding true.

My father paced the kitchen, plucking at his beard. Mairi and Seoras watched him, wide-eyed, huddled together on the bench. It was all I could do to keep still myself, and I could not stop my eyes from straying to the door, expecting at any moment to see it flung open, and the police burst into the room. Only Lachlann Ban appeared to be unconcerned, standing at ease by the fire, his hands thrust deep in his pockets, gazing down into the glowing red heart of the blazing peats. I marvelled at the queer quality of absolute stillness about him. He was as relaxed and self-contained as a cat, but the same one could move as swift as a cat when it suited him.

There was a sudden flurry of whistles, several blasting at once, and then another four in quick succession. The *bodach* stopped his pacing, and swung round on Lachlann

Ban. "I never heard tell of a police raid this early," he said. "In the dead o' night, yes, many's the time. But never this early." He resumed his anxious prowl, throwing words out as he went. "And if young Aonghas is right, and there are swarms o' them here, where did they come from?"

"Sheriff Ivory," I said. "The *Maighstir* told me the factor was after sending word to him the night o' the fire."

Mairi let out a squeal as the door burst open, and I must admit I was every bit as startled, seeing that I was up off the bench as if it had sprouted stinging nettles all of a sudden. I felt a right clown at the sight of Iain Beag and Eachunn Ruadh. But they had no eyes for me; it was Lachlann Ban their gaze was fixed on, and the look they gave him was without hope.

Eachunn Ruadh shut the door, and put his back to it. "The boy spoke true," Iain Beag said, his voice flat, and himself not an easy man to put down. "There is a ring o' lanterns about us, all the way from Coinneach's croft to the back of Old Diarmad's. I counted thirty-two o' them."

"Thirty-five by my count," Eachunn Ruadh put in.

Lachlann Ban whistled softly. "Likely there will be others without lanterns. Maybe more o' them guarding the bridge. Wi' the river on the flood they will know we could never cross by the stones. And we have got to cross the river if we are to breathe easy, boys. Once we are over the river, and the moor and the hills are ours to roam, I would not worry supposing an army was at our heels."

"What way can we get near the river?" Eachunn Ruadh demanded. "I am telling you, there is a ring o' them tight about us, and no way through unless we had wings."

Iain Beag nodded. "And three o' them are working up house by house. They are at Somhairle's."

Somhairle had the croft next to Coinneach. Two more houses to search, and that was them hammering at our door.

"Forty crofts in the township," my father said. "What made them start wi' this corner?"

"You may be sure Seamus Sionnach had a hand in it," Eachunn Ruadh said bitterly.

"Aye, it was never the work o' strangers," Iain Beag added. "I would not put it past that fox of a Seamus to have made off the minute he clapped eyes on Lachlann, and taken horse to Uig to acquaint the factor wi' the news. Easy done. Who would ha' noticed the going of him?"

One moment Lachlann Ban had been standing easy by the fire, looking as if he was near sleeping on his feet; the next he was pushing me aside, and pulling his canvas bag out from under the bench, slipping the knot that held it fast, and dragging out bundles of clothing. "Mairi," he said, without looking up, "make tea. Seoras, away out and fetch in some wet peats." He beckoned to the other three. "Get yourselves spread easy on the bench. Fill the *bodach's* pipe for him, Iain, and"—turning to my father—"get it drawing well, Alasdair. Eachunn, off wi' your boots and spread your stocking soles to the fire. I want it looking like you are all settled comfortable for the night, wi' no thought of even moving the length o' the stack-yard."

He held up a long black gown, and tossed it at me. "Into that, boy, and fast." The words were barely out of his mouth when he was pulling another stiff black gown over his head. The one I had on buttoned high at the neck and came down to my ankles. It was like preparing for the guising at Hallowe'en, and many's the Hallowe'en we had roamed the place dressed as women. Indeed, some of the carefree spirit of the guising took a hold of us. Mairi started to giggle every time she looked at me, and Iain Beag—more like his old self—declared, "It is as well we cannot make out or every man in the place would be chasing Alasdair, once they got a sight o' him in that rig."

"Wait you, till he gets his bonnet on," Lachlann Ban said. "That will be the making of him just." He handed Mairi a black bonnet, and drew the cord tight on his bag. "Get that tied about him, Mairi, and then hide my bag in the byre. Bury it in a stall among the cattle bedding. If they are city police, you may be sure they will never go near the beasts."

He drew on a close-fitting bonnet himself—one that covered the long scar on his cheek—and tied it carefully under his chin.

"Away on the stool behind the wheel," he said to me, pointing to the spinning-wheel in the corner. "Scoop your skirts under you when you sit. Aye, that is the way of it. And keep your face down. The bonnet hides it well, but if they get a right sight o' your nose that is us finished."

He picked up the wet peats that Seoras had brought in, and arranged two of them on the fire. Even with dry peats there was always a thick peat reek in the room, but with the smoke from the wet ones it would have taken a score of lanterns to pierce the gloom.

"Seoras," he said, "away to bed, and if strange men come pretend you are sleeping."

Seoras pulled back the ragged blanket that hid the box bed in a dark recess in the wall, and bolted in like a startled rabbit scuttling into the shelter of its burrow.

Lachlann Ban inspected the kitchen. He lifted the *cailleach's* knitting from the table, and settled down on her birch-bough stool in the far corner from the door. From where I sat behind the spinning-wheel, I would have sworn that the figure bent low on the stool was that of an old woman with her knitting on her lap—and if it came to the bit Lachlann Ban was as handy with the needles as any woman.

Mairi came back from the byre with news that she could hear voices raised in anger over at Tomas the Elder's, whose croft marched with our own. Tomas was not the man to be reckless at putting himself in bad with the police, but if they had burst in on him when he was kneeling at prayer he would speak as the spirit moved him.

"On wi' your chat," Lachlann Ban said. "There will not be a word out o' me and Alasdair from now on." He picked up the knitting, and the needles were soon clicking away good style, going that fast you would have thought he had been at nothing else all his days.

I set the wheel spinning, and what with the busy click of the needles, and the hum of the wheel, and the quiet voices of the men on the bench, and the sight of Mairi bent over the table buttering girdle scones, a stranger coming in on us would never have believed that we were expecting the police to hammer on the door any minute.

But there was no sudden knocking, not a sound. They must have crept up to the house, because the door was suddenly flung open without warning, and three monsters of policemen burst into the kitchen, like great black bats in their spreading cloaks and high, pointed helmets. Two of them carried lanterns, and all three had clubs in their fists.

Mairi had the big iron kettle in her hand. It slipped from her grasp, and the first of the three policemen got his boot caught up in the handle, and the thick serge of his trouser soaked in boiling water. That stopped his rush, and made him hop, I am telling you.

The fattest of the three—and he was the one without a lantern—looked about the kitchen, and said, "Alexander Stewart?"

I very near rose from my stool, clown that I was, thinking he had spotted me, fear so numbing my mind I had lost sight of the fact that he was speaking my father's name.

The *bodach* got up from the bench. The stance he took shielded me from their gaze, not that they could have seen much of my face the peat reek was that thick. "Alexander Stewart is my name," he said calmly.

One of the policemen had stayed with his back wedged firm against the door; the other had lifted the lid of the meal chest and was poking into it with his stick. "We are looking for your son of the same name," the fat one said.

If I had been in my father's boots, I swear that nothing on this earth could have stopped me from the folly of taking a quick look at the figure bent over the spinning-wheel. But the *bodach* never moved a whisker. "I doubt you are on the wrong side o' the hill," he said, as cool as you please. "My son is working over in Uig, at the inn."

"Your son was seen here to-day," the policeman said, letting his words sink home. That was Seamus Sionnach for sure, his tongue wagging fast to the factor. "Where is he?"

My father shrugged. "I told you. He is in Uig, working at the inn."

"You mean he was working at the inn. His master locked him in a room until he could be taken into custody, and he escaped." He lifted his arm, and patted his breast pocket. As his cloak fell away, I saw the stripes on the sleeve of his tunic. "I may tell you I hold a warrant for his arrest," he said. "If you are found harbouring the boy, it will be the worse for you."

My father shook his head, the way the right stupid do, who are that slow on the uptake their mind is still anchored fast on the first question long after others have been put in its place. "The boy is working in Uig," he repeated, "at the inn. That is all I know."

"Do you know a Lachlann MacGregor?"

"Aye, fine."

"I suppose you haven't seen him either."

The *bodach* shook his head.

"You haven't seen MacGregor?"

"Oh, I have seen him right enough."

"You have?"

"Amn't I after telling you I have?"

"When?"

"This afternoon. I saw him pull Tomas Fraser from the river, him that was helper to the sheriff officer."

"And where is he now?"

"Who knows?"

"I am asking you."

"And I am not knowing. But I would not wonder supposing he was the length o' the Red Point off Gairloch by now."

"Has he a boat?"

"He knows plenty who have."

"Have you seen him aboard a boat?"

"No, not me."

"Then what makes you think he is making for Wester Ross?"

"Well, he might have."

"Aye, and I might be home in my bed, and it a far cry

from this God-forsaken place." He took a note-book and pencil from his breast pocket, and glanced about the room. "I want the names of everyone here."

The *bodach* pointed to Mairi, her face full in the light of the lamp on the table. "My daughter, Mairi."

He turned to face Lachlann Ban. "Peigi Stewart," he said, "a cousin o' mine from Maligar. She was over at the *Maighstir* to——"

"*Maighstir?* What is the *Maighstir?*"

"The schoolmaster. She was over at him to get him to make a letter for her seeing she has no English. If you ask the *Maighstir* he will tell you she was in at him, and he——"

"Get on, man," the fat one snapped. "Do you think we are worrying about old wives too ignorant to put pen to paper?"

"But you said you wanted to know——"

"Their names, man, their names," the sergeant shouted. "Now, get on with it."

The *bodach* stepped aside, and jerked a thumb at me. "My cousin Peigi's daughter, Mairead. She reached over with her mother."

I sat with my hands folded tight in my lap, eyes downcast as the crawling seconds laid cold hands on my spine, every one stretching me taut on a terrible rack of apprehension. The only sound came from the busy *click, click, click* of Lachlann Ban's needles. In my mind's eye, I could see the dawning look of triumph on the fleshy face of the sergeant of police, hear his sharp summons to the other two, feel the bite of their grip as they seized my arms and dragged me struggling from the stool. Would Lachlann Ban be able to make a break for the door in the confusion?

I started, as the sergeant bellowed, "You two on the bench! Over here!"

The policeman who had been poking about in the meal chest held his lantern up to the faces of Iain Beag and Eachunn Ruadh, and lowered it near as swiftly. They must have been told that Lachlann Ban carried a scar on his left cheek that singled him out from other men. The sergeant took their names, and motioned them back to the bench, but not before the other fellow had satisfied himself that there was no one hidden under the bench.

The sergeant changed places with the man at the door. "Search the rest of the place," he ordered.

"I forgot Seoras," the *bodach* said. "My son, Seoras."

The words were barely out of his mouth when one of the policemen jerked the blanket aside from the wall-bed and thrust his lantern into the dark recess. Little Seoras let out a cry of terror, and drew back against the wall. "Where is your brother, boy?" the policeman said, bending over him.

I saw my father start forward, and I knew fine he was boiling. For one terrible moment, I thought he was going to hit the policeman. Lachlann Ban gave a loud sniff—and if I had closed my eyes I could have believed it was the *cailleach's* familiar sniff of disapproval. It pulled the *bodach* up short, but he let fly at the policeman with his tongue. "Are you wise, man," he cried, "frightening a boy the size o' Seoras, and him wi' no English?"

The policeman's fingers fastened around the stick that hung from a leather thong about his right wrist—and a right evil looking club it was; one blow would have been enough to strike a man senseless—and his eyes strayed to the sergeant at the door. I could not make out the look that passed between them, but the club was not raised. Instead he tried a laugh, saying, "If the Queen's English puts fear in the boy, you are needing civilising as bad as them Dervishes in the Soudan. A pity Mr. Gladstone ever sent General

Gordon to Khartoum, there was plenty work for him here."
He prodded the *bodach* in the chest with his stick, and made
for the door of the bedroom. But our father darted in front
of him, barring the way. "There is only my wife in there,"
he said, "and she is not well. I am not for having you
marching in on the mistress o' the house, and herself in
bed."

The big policeman seized him by his one good arm, and
flung him aside. It was strangely silent in the room, and
I realised that the busy clicking of Lachlann Ban's needles
had ceased. The *bodach* crashed back against the table,
making Mairi snatch at the toppling lamp. He recovered his
balance, and started forward again. But the policeman who
had scalded his leg pushed him aside, the way you would
swat a troublesome fly. The two of them strode into the
bedroom, their lanterns held high.

The *cailleach* let out a screech that could have been heard
on the other side of the river, and the sergeant called,
"Quieten your wife, man. If she is alone in the room, she
has nothing to fear."

That was easier said than done, but right enough the
racket she created speeded up the search. It was not long
before the two of them were back in the kitchen. They took
their time in the byre but they came back empty handed.

As they were all going out the door, the sergeant stopped
and turned to face my father. He stood there for that long
without speaking that if I had been the *bodach* I would have
felt forced to say something. But our father was wise enough
to stay dumb.

"We will be back," the sergeant said, "and if your boy was
mixed up in the murder of Fraser you had better say a prayer
for him. He will be needing it when Sheriff Ivory lays hands
on him."

Our father stood at the open door for long enough, staring after them. When he closed the door he motioned to us all to be quiet. He went into the bedroom, and I could hear his voice droning on at the *cailleach*, herself quiet for once, for a wonder. Mairi fed the fire with dry peats. When our father came back into the room, he stood looking down into the flames, and it was in me to believe—foolish as it may seem, and himself not a religious man—that he was making a prayer.

Iain Beag slipped out to scout the ground. He returned fairly dancing with glee. "We are clear o' them!" he crowed. "I was away down to the bridge, and I circled up the back as far as Old Diarmad's. There is not a sign o' life in the place."

Lachlann Ban rose from the low birch-bough stool, flexing his cramped limbs. He seized the *bodach* about the waist, and spun him off in a wild reel about the kitchen. Iain Beag hummed snatches of mouth music, the rest of us stamping out the time on the earthen floor. Lachlann Ban collapsed, laughing, on the bench, and what with the jests that were flying between us, the silence of the *bodach* went unremarked.

It is queer how the happiest of moods can come upon you at times of adversity, leaving you blind to the forebodings of others. When Lachlann Ban led the three of us out into the darkness of the night, I was wild at the *bodach* for coming after us, to see us clear of the croft as he said, and wilder still when he pulled me back under the rowan trees that grew thick about a rocky mound at the foot of the croft, where a house had stood in olden times.

"Watch yourself, boy," he whispered. "I have no fancy for the way this may end wi' the police speaking strong o' murder."

I told him I would watch myself, but it was the moon

I was watching, a beauty of a new moon hung fair above the black peak of Beinn Edra; that and the glittering swaths of light leaping about the heavens as the aurora set the northern sky dancing. In truth, I was near dancing myself, as I ran to catch up the others, my father's words forgotten the moment I left his side.

12

It was the year of the big frost, when the salt spray froze on the shore and the land stayed iron hard in the grip of the cold until April was come, that we had a plague of foxes. The tacksmen were losing that many sheep the factor had a notice posted in the shop offering a reward for every fox destroyed. Coinneach the Piper was a great fox hunter, and he did well that year. I was thirteen at the time, and I grew inches the day he took me with him.

We found a den high in the Quiraing, and I counted sixteen lambs' heads and the carcasses of grouse galore, curlews, wild duck, rabbits, hares, rats, mice and frogs, all within sight. We took cover, and settled down to wait. You had to be as patient as the fox, Coinneach said, and the fox had plenty patience.

It was near dawn when Coinneach spotted the white tip of the fox's brush, as he padded up the long gully to his den. He was moving up wind right enough, but the breeze was that light he could not have got our scent. Some sense of danger must have alerted him, though, because he stopped all of a sudden, well out of gunshot. And when he came on again it was in quick rushes from cover to cover, surveying every inch of ground from behind tufts of heather and fallen rocks, circling warily for a better sight of the way ahead.

He was almost within gunshot when he turned tail and streaked off, never stopping until he had climbed the next high ridge. Coinneach the Piper made the longest swear

I had ever heard in my life, and we got to our feet and took the weary trail home.

It was as well Coinneach had taken me with him that day, or I might have been tempted to ask Lachlann Ban why he did not make straight down the road to the bridge. He started off in the opposite direction, as if he was heading for the cliffs. Once we were on the other side of the dry-stone dyke that separated the arable lands of the township from the rough grazing, he swung round in a wide sweep to approach the bridge from the north, working his way upstream. Like the fox, he moved in quick rushes from cover to cover, and no fox ever spied the way ahead more warily.

Crouched behind an alder bush on the river bank, the roar of the spate loud in our ears, the three of us waited while he went on to scout the ground.

"A pity the flood did not come before Tomas Fraser went in the river," Eachunn Ruadh said.

"Ach, he would only ha' drowned the quicker." I looked down at the dark water creaming past the black rocks on its wild rush to the sea. "And maybe Lachlann Ban, too. No man could live in the like o' that."

"Aye, but Fraser's body would ha' been swept out to sea, and maybe never seen again," Eachunn Ruadh explained, in his slow, patient way.

"Supposing?"

Iain Beag poked me in the ribs. "Think on, boy. If there was no body, what way could the police charge Lachlann Ban wi' murder? You cannot have a murder without a body whatever."

Lachlann Ban ducked under the branches of the alder. If he had heard the talk of murder, he never let on. "The way seems clear," he said softly, "but we take no chances. If there are police on the watch sure enough they will be in one of the outbuildings o' the mill. We will walk over the bridge nice and easy and free o' care. When I give the word, run for it. If they make after us, scatter wide. We can meet up at the ruin of the old shepherd's hut above Marishadder."

The clatter of our boots on the bridge sounded that loud in my ears I thought we would waken the entire township. But not a soul stirred; not a light showed in the mill, huddled low like a great black beast suckling her young, alongside the far bank. Another two strides and we were over the river. "Run!" Lachlann Ban commanded, and the four of us sprinted past the mill, racing for the open moor.

We ran until a waste of moor lay between us and the bridge, and the roar of the river had diminished to a distant murmur. No human voice broke the silence, only the sharp cry of a hunting owl. Lachlann Ban slowed to a walk, and once he had got his breath back Iain Beag started to whistle a jaunty march.

It is queer how deceiving the moor can be. Viewed from our township, it lay like a great saucer between the river and the circling hills in the west, open to the eye and bare of shelter. But there were thousands upon thousands of hidden hollows where the hunted could lie secure in the heather, and an army search the ground in vain for a sight of them. Indeed, it is not an open place at all, the moor, but secret as the bed of the sea, every fold in the ground, every bank and stretch of bog offering a new place of concealment.

The farther we moved into the heart of the moor, the blither the step Lachlann Ban had on him. Mind you, I never saw the like of that man for moving without seeming haste, and covering ground at a fearful rate. He made you feel a laggard, it was that hard keeping up with him. His sure, strong stride never slackened, not even on the steep climb into the foothills where his way was barred by rushing burns, and the soft turf of the moor gave way to broken rock and scree.

I walked behind Lachlann Ban, following his footsteps and forcing my weary legs to keep pace with him. He led the way across a long gully in the hill, where the wind blew cold and strong as it channelled through the narrow funnel of rock. We squelched over long bare patches of black peat—the thin turf stripped clean by the force of the winter gales—wet and spongy underfoot, veined by coursing black streams. The track Lachlann Ban took wound around the rocky eastern face of Beinn Edra, and it was broken by treacherous scree that shifted under your boots and had to be crossed at a run. Iain Beag stopped his whistling.

The new moon lit the still pool of Loch Dubharsgoth far below, and then there was no chance of looking down, we were on a narrow ledge that wound around the shoulder of the hill under a looming overhang. One false step would have meant broken bones or worse, but to see Lachlann Ban footing it out you would have thought he had the whole wide moor secure beneath his boots.

A thin stream trickled down the furrowed hillside from a cleft in the rock face. Lachlann Ban squeezed his way into the narrow gap. I had no notion to follow him, but Iain Beag gave me an impatient push in the back.

The opening in the rock widened into a cave. Lachlann Ban had lit a candle, and I followed the flickering flame along a narrow passage in the rock, too narrow to admit the full span of Lachlann Ban's shoulders; he had to advance crabwise, one shoulder hunched forward. The long, narrow passage suddenly veered to the right widening into a great cavern that opened up in the bowels of the hill. A spring bubbled out of the rock, coursing across the sloping floor. Heaps of dry heather were scattered about the floor, and I stumbled into a pile of peats. Lachlann Ban slipped the canvas bag from his back. "No policeman ever reached this length," he said, "or likely to." His voice echoed eerily around the walls of the cavern.

In no time at all, Iain Beag had kindled a fire. Wherever the air came from, I knew not, but there was a beauty of a draught. The smoke went up as if we had bellows working, and the flames were soon leaping high. I took off my boots, and put my aching feet to the fire. Eachunn Ruadh spread dry heather at my back. "Stretch out, boy," he said, "there was never a better bed made for resting weary bones."

I lay back and closed my eyes, wondering idly why there was no peat reek in the cave. There must be some sort of natural chimney drawing the smoke clear. It was better than a hole in the thatch, that was a sure thing. Maybe there was a shaft clean through to the very peak of Beinn Edra. It was comical in a way to think of Beinn Edra puffing up a plume of peat reek, like a smoking volcano in foreign parts. Maybe folk would take fright thinking she was going to erupt.

The voices of the others lapped about me, falling away to a low murmur, like the sound of the sea when you put a shell to your ear. It was queer how their voices had changed, softening to a gentle hum, and them all close about me. It must be the cavern, shaped like the core of a giant shell. Maybe in the year 1985—and it a long, long century off; all that terrible weight of years to peel away and wither and die before it could be born—someone would put the cave to their ear and hear my voice.

I started up suddenly, crying, "The smoke! They will easy find us by the smoke!"

They were all gaping at me. Eachunn Ruadh said, "You must ha' been dreaming, boy."

"Never heed the smoke," Lachlann Ban said. "This is the secret place where the *bodachs* made the white whisky in olden days. Many's the fire burned bright here in days gone by, and many's the eye searched the hill for a trail o' smoke. The *bodachs* were not slow when they picked this place to brew the barley-corn. This cave has many a secret, and what happens to the smoke of a fire is one o' them. Rest easy, Alasdair. We could lie snug the long winter through while all the men o' the western world tramped the tackets off their boots seeking us out."

I yawned and stretched and lay back in the sweet smelling heather. Eachunn Ruadh had spoken true. It was a great bed. Iain Beag went to the spring to fill the kettle, but I was asleep before he got back to the fire.

When I awoke the flames were leaping high, and in those first moments of waking, my mind fuddled with sleep, I thought drowsily that the *cailleach* must have been early on the go seeing the fire was drawing so well. But there was no Seoras by my side; no familiar box bed. Memory flooded back, and I sat up, scrubbing at my eyes. Someone had thrown a thick plaid over me. I cast it aside, and scrambled to my feet.

The peat fire flames lit the heather beds; Lachlann Ban's canvas bag; a bundle of hazel sticks; a scatter of wood shavings and a black kettle. I peered into the darkness beyond the firelight. There was no sight or sound of the other three. The cave was empty.

"Lachlann!" I called softly, and the cavern whispered its mocking echo. "Lachlann!" I shouted, and the walls flung his name back at me: *Lachlann!*

He came running.

"Where were you?" I said.

"Taking my ease at our door." He gave me one of his rare smiles.

"Where is Iain?—Eachunn?"

"Out setting snares. A puckle o' meal and a poke of scones will not last us long."

"Is it night still?"

Lachlann Ban's laugh echoed around the cave. "Since when were you so sparing wi' sleep, boy? Good grief, it was near dawn before we landed here."

"What time is it, Lachlann?"

"Near two o'clock, boy—in the afternoon. Away and wash yourself, and I will make you a bowl o' brose."

I sluiced my bruised face with water from the spring. It was ice cold and had me chittering, but it cleared the sleep from my head something wonderful. I would need to ask Eachunn Ruadh on the quiet if he would give me a good kick the minute he woke, otherwise I was going to get a terrible name for sleeping.

When I had eaten, Lachlann Ban said, "Away and see the view from our door."

Standing in the narrow slit of the entrance to the cave was like being perched on the battlements of a giant castle, looking down on a pygmy world. The whole sweep of the coast stretching far to the south was spread out below, the townships tiny islands of green in the vast peaty brown ocean of moor.

I wondered, long afterwards, how I had ever spotted one moving speck in all that waste of hill and moor; one man moving steadily through the rocks and scree to the long, bare gully that was the start of the way to the cave. "Lachlann," I said, trying to mute the crow of triumph in my voice, "someone is making up the hill our way."

He followed my pointing finger, and he was not the man to waste words, Lachlann Ban. All he said was, "Come on."

He moved at such a pace I was well behind him when he came out of the long gully, and went sliding down a stretch of scree at breakneck speed. He stopped behind a huge boulder, and glanced back at me. I expected him to go on, but he waited until I had joined him. His pointing finger marked the climber below. "Your father," he said.

Well, he had some eyesight on him, Lachlann Ban. To me, the man below could have been almost anyone on two legs. But he was right enough. It was my father, and when we came together he was silent—and little wonder seeing the way Lachlann Ban stormed at him.

"Was I not after telling you to keep away," he cried, "and let the like of Aonghas take a message? Young an' all as he is the boy is in better trim for tackling the hill than yourself, and who would take heed of a boy that size? But let Seamus Sionnach catch a sight o' you making for the hill, and he would have the glass on you in a flash, and that is us finished."

"Seamus Sionnach is away to Uig," the *bodach* said heavily. "You know fine I would never make for the cave supposing there were eyes on me, and not then unless . . ." His voice tailed off, and he dug his boot into the thin turf as if he was striking at a mortal foe.

"Unless what?" Lachlann Ban said.

"Unless I had to."

"Well?"

The *bodach* sighed, and all of a sudden the words tumbled from him. "They came at first light. The sheriff officer and the police and a troop o' marines. We were all sleeping.

Colla heard her shouts and got word round, but what could we do? The marines had rifles—bayonets on them. They kept us back."

"Back?" Lachlann Ban said.

"Aye, back." Another stab of his boot into the ground. "They put your mother out. And, Lachlann—they fired the house, Lachlann."

There was a silence, and as sure as I am here I never want to breathe through another silence like that one.

"Where is the *cailleach*?" Lachlann Ban said.

"They took her to Portree. For questioning, they said. They cannot keep her, Lachlann. She has a sister in Skeabost. We sent word to her by the mail."

"And the cattle?"

"A drover is away wi' them. A stranger to me. I never clapped eyes on the man in my life."

"And you let him away?"

"Lachlann, what could we do? Four marines went along wi' him. What way could we stop them and themselves wi' rifles and bayonets at the ready?"

"Right enough," Lachlann Ban said, "you could not stand in the way o' rifles and bayonets." He drew a long breath, and set off down the hill at a great pace.

My father rushed after him, and seized him by the arm. "Wait, Lachlann, there is more. They say Sheriff Ivory will be off the boat in Portree to-night. They say there was word on the telegraph of his coming. And the word is that more marines are landing in Uig to-morrow, and Ivory is to be there when they come ashore. And the squad that was here this morning is camped in the Lodge."

"Let go o' my arm," Lachlann Ban said.

"But you cannot show face in the township, man. Supposing the marines are on the prowl? They are camped in the Lodge, I tell you. Or what if the police make over again? The only safe place for you is the hill."

"Safe or no, I am going," Lachlann Ban said. "Anyway, it will be near dark by the time we reach down."

It was dusk when we crossed the river by the old ford above Marishadder. The flood had fallen as quickly as it had risen. Not a word passed between the three of us as we climbed the drystone dyke, and came on the township from the south.

Seen from the distance in the near dark, the house looked the way it had always been. It was only when we came close we saw that the roof was open to the sky, the walls blackened with fire. A small figure stepped out of the shadows. It was Aonghas. The boy was near weeping. Lachlann Ban said, "Wait you, Aonghas, our day will come."

He stepped inside the ruined kitchen. The floor was littered with the remains of charred roof beams. The big iron cooking pot lay on its side. It was split clean in two. He toed it aside with his boot, and strode outside.

"What about the work you had for me, Lachlann?" Aonghas said.

"Monday, boy," Lachlann Ban replied, and his voice had a ring to it. "As sure as I am here, I have work for you on Monday."

We made back the way we had come, my father walking on ahead with Lachlann Ban—and it was Lachlann, I noticed, doing all the talking—Aonghas and me at their back. The trouble with Aonghas was his tongue was never still, and I could not catch a word of what was being said to my father.

We parted on the high moor beyond the township boundary, and as Lachlann Ban and I turned to go, I saw the glow of a fire in Valtos. "It is lit for the homecoming of Parnell," my father said. "Mr. Drummond the lawyer got him off this morning. He was found not guilty."

"I am not for lighting bonfires until the day I see Sheriff Ivory found guilty," Lachlann Ban said, "but that is one will never be brought to judgment in this world."

"Lachlann," the *bodach* said, seizing his arm as he made to go, "I know fine the way you feel, but if I were you I would think again. If you are wise, you will stay fast in the cave the day o' the rent collection."

"You know what I am needing," Lachlann Ban said, "and I am depending on you to have it ready for me." He took my father's hand in both of his. "Better to perish on our feet than live on our knees under the whip o' the factor."

He never said another word all the way back on the long climb to the cave, and although he told Iain Beag and Eachunn Ruadh what had happened they were no more successful than me in loosening his tongue.

All Saturday he was silent and withdrawn, and we woke on the Sabbath to find him gone. It was near dark when he came back, and he took his share of the rabbit stew in the same moody silence that had possessed him ever since he had learned of his mother's eviction.

But when he had finished eating, he got to his feet in one swift bound, and it was the old Lachlann Ban who faced us. "We have sat quiet long enough," he said. "The factor will be thinking he has us by the throat. Well, he is in for a surprise to-morrow. Listen, and I will tell you what we do."

13

The sky was patterned bright with stars when Lachlann Ban led us out on to the high eastern face of Beinn Edra. But the stars soon dissolved in a blur of tears as the bitter cold north wind stung my eyes like piercing needles. Indeed, I had not taken a score of paces when my teeth started to chatter that loud I was afraid the others would notice and think it was fear of what lay ahead that had me quivering from head to foot. But they were too intent upon shielding their faces from that demon of a wind to take heed.

I kept going by thinking of me and Seoras in the warmth of our box bed in the kitchen at home; gloating on the winter nights I had known when the gales beat about the house and I lay snug beside Seoras in the close company of the glowing peat fire.

I wondered if the others were thinking of the comfort of their beds at home, and then I remembered that all Lachlann Ban had was a ruin, standing open to the cold night sky and every chill wind that blew. Did you feel the cold worse when you had no corner of your own to lay your head, or was it all one? Well, I should know. When would I rest in my own bed again? How could I know from one night to the next where I was going to lay my head? Supposing Lachlann Ban's plans went awry, it could be the hard floor of a prison cell for me before the day was done. Well, I would rather sleep out in the open on the bleak

face of Beinn Edra than that. It must be terrible to hear a
key turn in the lock, and know that was you held fast within
four stone walls, no bigger than a cattle stall, until a stranger
took the notion to come along and release you. What if
they forgot, or all the turnkeys died in the night? What if
your cries went unheeded, and day after day after day the
door never opened?

It is queer how the mind is the master of the body. I was
near perished with the cold, my hands numb, feet that
frozen they felt like lumps of unyielding rock, but I swear I
started to sweat.

The first light of dawn was starting to flush the eastern
sky above the hills of Wester Ross as we reached down to the
river. We crossed by the old ford, and Lachlann Ban
quickened his pace, climbing fast up the shelving ground
to the high moor above Ellishadder. As we neared the
road, he motioned the rest of us down, and went on alone
as we flattened into the heather. He was back in the blink
of an eye, and we were up again and running across the
road, not stopping until we were safely over the first ridge
and hidden in a hollow.

We circled the boundary of Old Diarmad's croft, skirting
the high outcroppings of rock that would have brought us
within sight of the road, and working out towards the cliffs
before we swung back and made for the deep saucer of the
peat bog that lay at the back of our township.

The ground was criss-crossed with the long straight lines
of the peat cuttings, most of them stripped bare, the hard-
won harvest long since carted home. One of the cuttings
with a stack of peats still to be moved was my father's.
There was a cart standing on our bog, its long shafts reaching
up over the top of the stack; a dun-coloured pony grazing
at the end of a long tether nearby. I knew the face of the

pony as well as that of any man in the place; she belonged to Eachunn Ruadh's father. But a stranger could never have picked her out from the score or more of duns in the township. And as for the cart, there was nothing to mark it out from any other cart in the place.

Aonghas must have been watching for us from the rocks above the drystone dyke. He came bounding down the slope, meeting us as we reached my father's bog.

"I am the only one up in the whole place," Aonghas said proudly. "There is not a light to be seen, not even about the Lodge. Do you suppose the soldiers are sleeping, Lachlann? If there was a war on, we could capture them easy."

The words were barely off his lips when a bugle call sounded. We turned as one, and raced up the slope to the rocks. Another bugle call rang out, distant but clear. Every eye lifted to the jagged peaks of the Quiraing. Lachlann Ban was the first to spot them. "Marines," he said, "coming down through the pass."

We waited, crouched behind the rocks, watching the long line of men wending down to the plain; waited until they passed out of sight between the trees that lined the road to the Lodge.

"Three score o' them," Eachunn Ruadh murmured, "at the very least."

"Time we were moving," was all Lachlann Ban said.

And move he did, working swiftly to strip the top layers of peats from the stack. He uncovered the pony's harness and a bundle of birch boughs. While the rest of us harnessed the pony to the cart, he was busy fitting the birch boughs into place. They had all been cut to length, so that by bending them in the fashion of a bow they made a wedge fit in the box of the cart.

Lachlann Ban built a frame half the length of the box,

and the rest of us stacked it with a roof of interlocking peats a good six deep.

"Right, boys," he said, unrolling the long black gown he had carried with him, and pulling it over his head, "in you go."

Eachunn Ruadh, Iain Beag and I crawled under the birch bough frame, and Aonghas started to toss peats into the back of the cart. Lachlann Ban pulled on a close-fitting bonnet, and once he set to work with Aonghas the three of us were soon enclosed by peats.

The cart jolted forward, showering peat dust down on us as it bumped over the rough track that wound out of the bog and across the moor to the road. We knew when we had reached the road; there were no more sudden lurchings, flinging us into one another as a wheel caught in a rut, or bone-shaking jarrings as the cart plunged down into a gully.

It was no more than two miles to the Lodge but it was the longest two miles I ever travelled. When the cart finally stopped and the first pin-point of light penetrated the darkness of our prison it was as much as I could do to lie still as Lachlann Ban had ordered.

The first thing I saw was the split uppers of Aonghas's boots. He was standing in the back of the cart tossing out peats as fast as he could go. Lachlann Ban's face came over the tailboard. He had only to say the one word to get us moving.

We wriggled out from under the frame and slid stiffly off the cart. It had been backed into a fuel shed facing the kitchen quarters of the Lodge. The jutting gable end of the building hid us from the yard, but I could hear the tramp of heavy boots on the cobbles and the sound of English voices.

"The stables are round on the right," Lachlann Ban said

to Iain and Eachunn. "March in as if you owned the place, mind." There were two pails in the shed; he snatched them up. "Here, take a pail apiece. If any o' the marines says a word to you, make out you have no English."

As they went off, he said to Aonghas, "Be sure and clear all the birch boughs out o' the cart, Aonghas. You should be back home before anyone in the township has stirred." And to me: "Gather an armful o' peats and follow me."

"Lachlann," Aonghas wailed, tugging vainly at one of the wedged birch boughs, "I am not able to shift them."

Had a hostile eye chanced to look in at that moment we were done for. Even the most unsuspecting would have questioned the sight of an old *cailleach* gathering up her skirts and leaping lightly into the back of the cart, big hands snatching at the bent ribs of birch and wrenching them clear of the box.

Lachlann Ban jumped to the ground, and dusted down his skirts. He crossed to the Lodge, head bowed, feet dragging slow, and I was at his back, only my eyes visible above a great armful of peats.

He opened a door at the back, and I followed him along a short, stone-flagged passage into the kitchen. Peigi, Coinneach the Piper's daughter, was down on her knees lighting the range. It was not until Lachlann Ban pulled off his bonnet that she recognised him, and then she could not get to her feet for laughing. While he was struggling out of his long black gown, and trying to stop her giggles and tell her what she had to do, I dumped the peats in a wicker basket, and got down on my knees in Peigi's place and coaxed the fire into a quick blaze.

She took us out of the kitchen by a second door, led us along another passage, pushed open a swing door covered with green stuff, soft to the touch, and across a wide, tiled hall to the room where the rent collection was to be held.

It was a huge room with a high, plaster ceiling and tall windows looking out across the bay. There was another big window in the wall opposite the door, both of them draped with heavy velvet curtains that hung the length of the floor. A long table was arranged across the centre of the room, three chairs standing out from it, their backs to the fire. There was another small table, sparkling with fancy inlay, in the corner between the windows, and a straight-backed chair with queer curving legs in the other corner by the door. The wall beyond the door was filled by the biggest sideboard I had ever clapped eyes on.

Lachlann Ban took out his knife, and stepped behind the curtains facing the table. I watched him cut a slit in them at eye level. He guided me behind the curtains at the other window, and slit them for me so that I could watch the door. "I will have my eyes fixed on the three at the table," he said, "so you will need to watch the door. At the first sight o' trouble, give a sharp whistle."

"How do you mean, trouble?" I said.

"Maybe Iain and Eachunn brought to the door wi' chains on them," he said grimly. "Use your eyes, boy, and whistle sharp to give me warning."

I nodded. "What now, Lachlann?"

"We wait behind the curtains," he said. "Peigi has got a right roarer of a fire going, so take care you are not sleeping."

That was easy done. I would have stayed awake for a week for the chance of seeing Seamus Sionnach's face when Lachlann Ban emerged from behind the curtains.

The factor was the first one through the door, followed by his clerk, a brass bound cash box under one arm, and the big ledger containing the rent roll clutched under the other. Seamus Sionnach trailed behind them, looking like a cat that has just tasted cream after a long drouth. "What did I tell you, Major?" he crowed, rubbing his hands in glee. "There is a queue o' them at the door since hours, they are that eager to get in and pay the rent."

The factor lifted his coat tails and put his backside to the fire. "Well, get on, man, have them called in."

I wish you could have seen their faces when Lachlann Ban stepped out from behind the curtains with a pistol in his fist! The clerk was bent over the table just about to take his seat, and he flopped into the chair as if the legs had been cut from under him. The factor's hands came out from behind his coat tails, and he took one quick step forward. Just the one. Like a man suddenly realising there is a wall facing him. Seamus Sionnach's face underwent the best change of all. It was as if he had been caught in a boat, one not making way at all, and rolling beam on in a heavy swell—and himself not a good sailor. The colour drained from his face, and it changed from a pasty grey to a sickly green. He never moved, but his big Adam's apple was up and down like a storm-tossed cork.

"Sit you down," Lachlann Ban said, waving the pistol carelessly at the two of them.

The factor took the centre chair. Seamus Sionnach was rooted fast between the table and the door. A wave of the pistol and he scutttled to the chair on the factor's left.

Lachlann Ban advanced to the table, and tapped it gently with the barrel of the pistol. *Tap, tap, tap*. Three pairs of eyes followed the movements of the pistol.

"You know me," he said, turning his face to the factor, and running a finger slowly down the long scar on his cheek. "I carry your mark, and it is one I will carry to the grave. And you know fine I would welcome the chance o' putting my mark on you. So heed what I say.

"When the first man appears before you, and the clerk tells him what he has to pay, you will ask him how much money he has in his house, and how much he is owing at the shop. If he is giving all he has to you, you will tell him he can hold back the rent until times are better."

The factor licked his lips. "There are almost a hundred marines here. A guard of police and marines at the gates, watching everyone who passes in and out. Marines patrolling the walls. I would advise you to give yourself up now, and I will use my influence to see that you are treated with mercy."

"You forget this mark o' yours," Lachlann Ban said, tapping his cheek. "Supposing I put a different kind o' mark on you? Not such a bad one, maybe, not one that every man would see on sight, but bad enough. Supposing I put this pistol to your knee and pulled the trigger? You would limp bad for the rest o' your days, Major Traill."

"He would do it, the same one," Seamus Sionnach yelped.

The factor's fleshy face had lost its ruddy glow. "You will never get away with this," he asserted. "It—it is an outrage."

Lachlann Ban leaned across the table, the pistol rock steady in his hand, not six inches from the major's white face. "Is it not an outrage to fire the house of an old woman, and herself a widow? Is it not an outrage to seize her cattle, and drag her from her hearth in the dark o' night? Watch your words, Major Traill, or I am telling you I will put an end to the talk, and have done wi' you once and for all."

"Very well," the factor said, speaking as if he was biting on broken glass, "I will do as you say."

"And you," Lachlann Ban snapped, turning on the cowering Seamus Sionnach, "translate true into the English whatever they tell you. I will be listening, mind. Now, summon them in."

He backed to the curtain, and stepped behind it. Seamus Sionnach got up, and walked to the door like a drunk man. He opened the door, and called that the rent collection was starting.

The first man in was Old Diarmad, his bonnet clutched in his fist. Seamus Sionnach spoke his name, and the clerk tracked him down in the big ledger. "Rent, £12," he said. "Arrears, £29. 10. 6."

Old Diarmad put his bonnet on the floor, and took a purse out of his pocket. He tipped the contents on to the table, and the clerk quickly sorted it into two heaps. Ten gold sovereigns and three five shilling pieces. "I am not able for more," Old Diarmad said in Gaelic to Seamus Sionnach.

"He says that is all he can manage," the ground officer told the factor.

Major Traill's eyes strayed to the window overlooking the bay. "Ask him what money he has in his house," he snapped, "and if he is in debt at the shop."

When Seamus Sionnach put the question to him, Old Diarmad scratched his head. "Money?" he said. "What money? You see it all there." He pointed to the table.

"And what of the shop?" Seamus Sionnach said. "Are you owing at the shop?"

"What man is not?" Old Diarmad said. "But there is many a one in this place worse in debt than me."

"How much are you owing?"

"Near six pounds."

"And have you no money in the house?"

"The money I have is there," Old Diarmad said, pointing to the table. "Amn't I after telling you I am not able for more?"

When the factor had been told, his gaze flickered from the window to the door. He licked his lips. "Tell him," he said stiffly, "he can keep his money until he is in a better position to pay the rent."

Seamus Sionnach told him, and the old man saluted the three of them in turn, starting with the factor, and saying, "Thank you, gentlemen," three times over. He was in such a daze he had to be called back twice, once to collect his money from the table, and a second time to lift his bonnet from the floor.

One after another they filed into the room, and answered the ground officer's questions; and one after another they went out again with their purses unopened. When Peigi wheeled in loaded trays of food for the three behind the table, it near killed me to see so many good things going to waste, their appetite was that poor.

All afternoon the men made their way into the Lodge for the rent collection, and there was not one who did not take away with him the money he had brought to pay the rent. The light was failing, and the clerk had newly lit the oil lamp on the table, when Peigi came in with a tray of tea, and the news that there were no more waiting at the door. I wondered what had happened to my father; the *bodach* had not shown face all day.

"Take that tray away, girl," the factor snapped. "You can bring tea when I ring for it, and not before."

"Yes, sir," Peigi said, that meek you would never have guessed she had been obeying the instructions of Lachlann Ban. She gave the factor a quick bob, and picked up the tray, and hurried out.

Lachlann Ban stepped out from behind the curtains. "Away to the door, Alasdair," he said.

I ran to the door, and gripped the handle. Lachlann Ban

faced the three of them at the table. "Take your time about following us," he said quietly. "If I get a sight of any one o' you on the other side o' that door, I will blast a hole clean through you."

They were silent as he backed to the door, covering them with his pistol. "Open it, Alasdair," he whispered, "and run for the front door—straight across the hall."

I got the door open, and ran. Lachlann Ban was right behind me as I fumbled at the handle of the big double door and wrenched it open.

The laird's coach, with his four jet-black ponies between the shafts, was standing at the door. The black-coated coachman, in his tall hat, was holding the bridles of the lead ponies. As he turned, I saw the anxious face of Iain Beag under the tall hat. Eachunn Ruadh catapulted out of the back of the coach. The two of them drew their knives and slashed the traces holding the ponies to the shafts. Iain Beag lost his hat scrambling on to the back of a pony, but we were all mounted and away before the first shouts issued from the Lodge.

We swept down the drive, Lachlann Ban and myself in the lead, and we were through the gates before the startled guards were aware of what was happening. I got a good grip on my pony's long mane, and dug my heels into his flanks. He went up the winding path to the main road like the wind, a good length in front of Lachlann Ban's mount and the four of us tore through the township at full gallop. We did not ease our sweating beasts to a canter until we were through the township gate, and on the road to Ellishadder.

Lachlann Ban led the way off the road, wheeling across the moor at a gentle trot. We forded the river on horseback, and did not dismount until we had ridden into the foothills.

The four ponies settled down to graze, but by the time another day had dawned they would have wandered miles away.

We rested in the shelter of a green hillock until the gathering dusk had turned to dark. There were lights galore to be seen about the road and moving up and down from the Lodge. If they were searching for us they would have sore feet before they were done.

I looked at Lachlann Ban, sprawled on his stomach, his keen eyes intent upon the lights far below. He had got into the Lodge and out again, as he had said he would, and saved everyone in the place from a winter of want. If only my father had been there to see it for himself. I wondered why the *bodach* had not shown face at the rent collection. Everyone else in the place had obeyed Lachlann Ban, and put in an appearance.

He called us to our feet, and we started off again. The wind had veered to a southern quarter; I could smell the rain in the air. When we reached the heights the mist was swirling thick about the crags, black peaks suddenly emerging from the smoking vapour only to vanish as swiftly again.

The other three had let me take the lead, joking that I would never find the cave in the mist. I found it right enough, and sprinted on ahead of them. As I rounded the bend in the narrow passage that led into the great cavern, the flames from a good going fire lit my way. I went on for half a score of paces—I was that slow on the uptake— before I stopped, wondering stupidly how a fire came to be burning when we had left the cave hours before daybreak.

My father rose from the shadows and came to meet me. But I had no eyes for the *bodach*. My gaze was fixed on the smallest man I had ever clapped eyes on; a perfectly formed little manikin, in a tight fitting black coat and city boots that would near have fitted my little brother Seoras. He was standing by the fire and he had his back to the blaze in the same manner as the factor, his coat tails flipped over his linked hands. And Major Traill himself could not have given me a less welcoming look.

14

"Mr. Drummond," my father said, squinting down at his boots, shrivelled by the look Lachlann Ban had given him on finding a stranger in the cave, and that stranger a lawyer man, "got Parnell clear o' the jail on Friday." His eyes lifted from his boots, and scanned the faces of the four of us. "I was thinking you all might be the better of a word with him."

"Aye, maybe so," Lachlann Ban allowed, "if we were behind bars in the grip o' the law. But I am as well acquaint wi' this stretch o' hill as I am with the hand I see before me." He examined his strong right hand, slowly balling it into a fist, and although he looked across at my father, I knew fine his words were addressed to the lawyer. "And if what you say is right enough about Sheriff Ivory offering the police medals for our capture, it only goes to show the man is desperate. I am telling you, there is not a policeman born will take me on this hill."

"But Mr. Drummond can explain things," my father pleaded, casting an anxious glance at the lawyer, who had never opened his mouth so far. "Mr. Drummond knows what is doing away from here. There are big changes coming wi' the General Election in December. Mr. Gladstone is sure to be——"

"Mr. Gladstone!" Lachlann Ban exploded. "The same one was Prime Minister at the time o' the Royal Commission. It was Mr. Gladstone sent us the Queen's Commissioners

to look into our grievances. They were long enough report-
ing, and what did they say? Were we to get security from
eviction? No. Was the Government to take a look at the
rents the factors were after forcing out of us? No. All they
could say was that a good half of us would be the better
of clearing out o' the place and taking ship for foreign
parts. Mr. Gladstone is not worried about this place, nor
Lord Salisbury either. It is Ireland has them worried, and
I will tell you for why. The Irish have guns, and they are
not afraid to use them."

"Ach, you must listen, Lachlann," my father said, anguish
in his voice. "Mr. Drummond can help you."

"Not in any professional way," the little lawyer said, and
I was thunderstruck by the voice that issued from that wee
man; a great boom of a voice, every bit as deep as the voice
of Colla the smith. "Not as a lawyer, you understand, not
unless you cease your lawless acts and face your accusers in
a court of law." He lifted his gloved hands as Lachlann Ban
made to speak, adding, "I am here privately—shall we say,
as a friend?"

Lachlann Ban looked from Iain Beag to Eachunn Ruadh;
and another angry glare went my father's way from him.
He shrugged. "Say what you will."

"Well, as one interested in reform, I must say you are not
assisting the cause of those you wish to help."

"What does that mean?" Lachlann Ban's voice never
rose, but I did not fancy the look in his eye. If I had been
the wee man, I would not have stopped to answer.

"It means," he boomed, his great voice sounding strong
about the cavern, the echo ringing back, "you are the
best friend Sheriff Ivory has in the Highlands of Scotland."

It was his size that saved him. If he had been built like a normal man—or on the giant scale of Colla the smith—I believe Lachlann Ban would have smashed him down where he stood. But angry and all as he was—and he was white about the lips—he could not bring himself to lay hands on such a wee cratur. "Me? A friend of Sheriff Ivory!" he exclaimed, near choking on the words, the rage he had on him was that great. "If I could lay hands on Sheriff Ivory I would squeeze the life out of him."

"Exactly," the lawyer said, "I could not have put it better myself. If you persist in this attitude, Sheriff Ivory can claim—with no little justification—that he is dealing with lawless brigands who must be subdued by force of arms. Even those who would question most strongly the use the sheriff has made of his office to support unjust actions by some landlords—even those eager sympathisers of the crofters' cause shrink from appearing to support acts of violence. And if your friends feel that way, how can you expect the Government of Lord Salisbury in London to restrain Sheriff Ivory?"

"Lord Salisbury or Mr. Gladstone," Lachlann Ban said, "it is all one. They are not caring what goes on in this place."

"You cannot expect them to listen to you," the lawyer said sharply, and I marvelled at the nerve of him. "So long as you are engaged in acts of violence and destruction of property, it is Sheriff Ivory who will have their ear."

"To pot with Sheriff Ivory!" Lachlann Ban cried. "He will be glad to clear back to Inverness before I am done wi' him."

"I fear you are in some ignorance of the forces being assembled against you," the wee man said. "There is normally only one telegraph clerk in Portree, but on

Saturday a special staff arrived with a Wheatstone Automatic Transmitter. If the Post Office is expecting such heavy traffic on the telegraph, Sheriff Ivory must be planning to increase the scale of his operations here—and you are making it easy for him."

And you are making it easy for him. If ever words in their passage acquired the stinging tails of scorpions those words did. I could not bring myself to look at Lachlann Ban. But he was off, striding the length of the cave, his back to the lawyer. When he returned, all he said was: "Tell me how I am making it easy for Sheriff Ivory."

"Certainly," the lawyer said, not in the least abashed by the daggers of looks he was getting. "Sheriff Ivory has been pressing the Government for troops since last August. Those of us who knew made it clear to the Government that he would use the military to enforce the serving of notices of eviction on crofters who could not pay their rent. That is why he did not get them. There would have been an outcry unless the troops were also used to compel the landlords to pay their rates. You may not think this is so," he went on quickly, seeing the look on Lachlann Ban's face, "but in law even great lairds like Lord MacDonald could have their property seized for non-payment of rates and taxes just the same as the crofter's cattle and few sticks of furniture. The law takes no account of the social station of a debtor. But Sheriff Ivory has got his troops now. There are more on the way. And he has got them because of the disorders you have provoked. He will use them as he sees fit, always claiming that he is upholding the law. And who can say him nay in London, when it is the duty of a Government to maintain law and order?"

"But it was Lachlann that saved everyone in the place to-day," I burst out, in the silence that followed. "If it had not been for Lachlann they would have had the last penny dragged out o' them at the rent collection."

"By holding a pistol to the factor's head?" the lawyer said. "Dear me, that is no solution to the problem. The factor can call another rent collection next week—to-morrow, if he pleases—and the people will have to present themselves, and make payment."

"When there are hundreds ready to swear on oath the factor himself told them they could hold back the rent until they were better able to pay?" Lachlann Ban roared. "Is the law to take the word o' the factor and his clerk and that rag of a ground officer against the sworn word o' hundreds? None o' the crofters laid eyes on me. None o' them knew I was there wi' a pistol in my fist. I was hid behind the curtains."

"I am afraid you are a little confused," Mr. Drummond said, hitching his coat tails behind him, and surveying us for all the world like a *Maighstir* in miniature about to give his scholars a right dressing down. "Whether they saw you or not is of no concern. Whether the factor acted under duress or not is equally of no concern. In law, the factor is free to tell his debtors they may withhold payment, and the very next day to demand payment in full from them. However well intentioned your efforts may have been—and from what I understand of the affair you appear to have behaved like a Corsican brigand—you have not prevented the factor from demanding payment of all rents due to the estate."

There was a stunned silence. My father was busy studying his boots. Eachunn Ruadh and Iain Beag had their eyes on Lachlann Ban, willing him to speak. The silence was more than I could bear. "What would you ha' done?" I cried, heedless of the quick lift of my father's head and the angry glare he directed at me, "have them hand over their last penny and see the winter through wi' limpets off the rocks?"

"I would have sought the removal of the military," he said calmly, not in the least put up or down by my outburst. "With the military out of the way, I have no doubt the people could resist the more oppressive demands made upon them."

"You must first get rid o' the man who brought them here," Lachlann Ban countered.

The little man nodded. "As a matter of fact, I am in process of bringing about his removal from office, unless you succeed in convincing the Government that so lawless a part of the realm is in need of a law officer as harsh as Sheriff Ivory."

"You are to get rid o' Sheriff Ivory?" Lachlann Ban said slowly—and it was a credit to us that not one of us burst out laughing.

"My client," the lawyer said. "Mr. Norman Stewart— Parnell as you call him."

"What is Parnell doing?" Lachlann Ban scoffed. "Making up a letter to the papers? The like o' Parnell is meat and drink to Sheriff Ivory. He would make a meal o' the same one before breakfast."

"My client was found not guilty on a charge of mobbing and rioting," Mr. Drummond said crisply. He stripped off his gloves and produced a folded sheet of newspaper from an inner pocket. "Sheriff Ivory wrote to the Lord Advocate," he went on, bending over the flames to see the better, "in these terms: 'We apprehended Norman Stewart, alias Parnell, the leading ringleader of the mob and the principal promoter of the lawless proceedings in the district.'

"That was a confidential communication, of course, but

Sheriff Ivory was misguided enough to communicate it to a newspaper, and his words have appeared in the public prints. As my client was found not guilty of lawless behaviour, Sheriff Ivory has committed a libel on him. My client is now raising an action claiming damages for libel. We will win—and the outcome will be the resignation of Sheriff Ivory from the Sheriffdom of Inverness, Elgin and Nairn."

"Who is going to make the like o' Sheriff Ivory resign?" Lachlann Ban demanded.

"The law," the little man said simply. "The law which demands impartial justice of those charged with its administration." He flicked a speck of peat ash off his coat sleeve. "It will be the end of the reign of Sheriff Ivory."

That took some digesting, and there was a silence as we chewed on it. Mr. Drummond took a few dainty steps about the floor. I wondered how those wee legs of his had managed the long climb to the cave. He was tougher than he looked. Well, he would need to be, if he had the beating of Sheriff Ivory.

"You know," he boomed, swinging round on Lachlann Ban, "you and your friends are a confounded nuisance to me. I have no doubt I will be defending you all in court one day, and precious little hope I shall be able to offer you. And of course, it will be a bad day for your cause if the charges laid against you are ever heard in court."

He did another little turn up and down the floor, hands locked behind the tails of his coat. "I believe you were once considering emigrating to the United States, Mr. MacGregor. I would think about it again, if I were you. And your friends might find the climate there much more congenial America is a big country. You would all have room for your—ah—undoubted energy." He turned to

my father. "Come, Mr. Stewart, I am no expert moun-
taineer, and we have an arduous descent before us."

The three of us followed himself and the *bodach* to the
start of the narrow passage at the end of the cave. Mr.
Drummond held out his tiny gloved hand to Lachlann Ban.
It was swallowed entire in Lachlann's big fist.

"I have seen your mother," he said. "She is lodged with
her sister in Skeabost, and is well. I will be contesting the
poinding of her cattle in due course." He looked at Eachunn
Ruadh and Iain Beag, appraising each in turn, before turning to Lachlann Ban. "And I have spoken to the parents of
your friends. They all have the same message: Go, and go
quickly."

"And the place crawling wi' marines and police ready to
pounce once we come down from the hill?" Lachlann Ban
said.

The lawyer shrugged. "Pray remember that once Sheriff
Ivory takes command—and he will be here once he
receives news of to-day's proceedings—he will soon have
you circled by a ring of redcoats. Every pass, every track,
every bridge will be watched and guarded. It would be
excessively foolish of you to make it too easy for your hunters
to earn their medals."

"Aye, Lachlann," the *bodach* said eagerly, "Mr. Drummond is right enough." His strong left hand gripped mine,
and I was proud of the smile he gave the pair of us. "Better
a new life in America," he said, with a laugh, "than an old
prison on the mainland."

But his fingers clung to my hand as if they would never
let go.

15

"Do you reckon that wee cratur can get rid o' Sheriff Ivory?" Iain Beag said, breaking fresh peats across his knee, and building the fire up under the cooking pot. Not stopping for an answer, he went on, "I am not big myself, but the lawyer man is that wee it is a wonder he is ever seen in the courts, unless he has a chair to stand on."

"He is not needing to be seen," Lachlann Ban said, "not wi' that big voice on him."

"And he said it was all Parnell's doing," Eachunn Ruadh added. "Parnell is a great hand at the letter writing right enough, but I never thought he would have the nerve to tackle Sheriff Ivory. There is brains in the family, but where did he get the learning for that kind o' work? That libel thing the wee man was on about."

"An action for libel is what he called it," I said.

Eachunn Ruadh shook his head in wonder. "He has a nerve on him, Parnell, doing the like o' that."

"It is not Parnell's doing," Lachlann Ban corrected him. "That was lawyer's talk just, all that palaver about my client this, and my client that. It is all the work o' the wee man, Eachunn. Parnell could be gagged and blinded, it would not make a mite o' difference. The wee lawyer man stands at his back, and he is not only loading the pistol, he is firing the shots as well."

"Even supposing," Eachunn Ruadh said, "I do not see how this libel thing can work. What is it, anyway?"

"Making lies on a person," Iain Beag told him, "and spreading them thick about the place."

Eachunn Ruadh laughed. "It was a lie right enough, making out that Parnell was leading the fight against the factor. But how can that wee lawyer man get rid o' Sheriff Ivory just because he was making lies on the like o' Parnell?"

He was slow on the uptake, Eachunn Ruadh, but I left it to Lachlann Ban to spell it out for him. "Supposing Mr. Gladstone was caught riding on a tram in the city without paying his fare," Lachlann said.

"Ach, Mr. Gladstone would never do a thing like that," Eachunn Ruadh declared. "Besides, he has plenty money."

"But supposing he did," Lachlann Ban insisted.

"Well, the disgrace would be something terrible. That would be him finished for the job o' Prime Minister, supposing the Liberals get in at the Election. You could not have a Prime Minister riding the trams and not paying his fare."

"Well then," Lachlann Ban said "if Mr. Drummond wins the case for Parnell that is the great Sheriff Ivory humbled by a poor crofter and himself disgraced. The Government is not going to stand for the like o' that. An officer o' the law—and a mighty one!—caught telling lies! It is worse than a shepherd stealing sheep, Eachunn."

"You reckon the wee cratur will win?" Iain Beag asked him.

"Aye, he will win right enough," Lachlann Ban declared. "He is smart, the wee man, and hardy. It would take more than Sheriff Ivory to make him draw back."

"And if he manages to get rid o' Sheriff Ivory, what then?" Iain Beag was smart enough, too, when it came to the bit.

Lachlann Ban took his time replying. "If he gets rid o' Sheriff Ivory," he said slowly, "the like o' Major Traill will not find it so easy to get the law come running whenever he cracks his whip. For any favour, there is not the equal o' Sheriff Ivory in the length and breadth o' Scotland."

"So maybe Mr. Drummond spoke true saying it would be as well for us to get clear o' the place," Iain Beag went on. "Me, I am not fancying the jail at all, at all—even supposing we have the wee man speaking up for us—but I have a right notion for America."

"Aye, and me," Eachunn Ruadh said.

Lachlann Ban turned to me. "What about you, Alasdair?"

The question caught me unawares. In truth, I did not know what to say, but words sprang unbidden to my lips. "Well, there is one thing sure," I heard myself say, "Sheriff Ivory would be wild if we got clear—and we would be free o' the redcoats in America."

"Aye, supposing we vanished he would look a right fool," Lachlann Ban mused, "summoning an army, and themselves busy hunting shadows. And if we managed the length o' Glasgow, Mr. George would see that we got a ship to America. But how do we get clear, and the place crawling wi' marines? That will take some thinking out, I am telling you."

We had plenty of time for thought. The mist came down in the night, and the next morning you could barely see your hand in front of your face outside the cave. We were shut in by great swirling banks of dense vapour that penetrated the innermost corners of the cavern, and made the fire burn dim.

It was the same the next day, and the day after that; the mist settled so thick about the crags we could not get out to the snares. On the third day all we had to eat was a handful of meal apiece, and long before night came the only sound in the cavern was the rumbling of our empty bellies.

Lachlann Ban could not keep still. He was up and down, up and down, restlessly pacing the floor of the cavern, that moody and withdrawn none of us dared speak to him. Even Iain Beag was sunk in gloom by the third day, tight-lipped and touchy. When Eachunn Ruadh kept on at him about what a blessing it was having such a good spring in the cave, seeing a man could live for long enough if only he had plenty of water to drink, Iain Beag let fly such an angry swear at him that the two of them very near came to blows. It was queer how our refuge had become a prison all of a sudden.

But Friday dawned bright, with the wind away to the north-west, and clouds white as the wool of fresh sheared sheep scudding about the clear blue sky. Iain Beag and Eachunn Ruadh hurried off to the snares, their quarrel forgotten, and Lachlann Ban took me with him on a scouting expedition.

He kept to the west side of the high crags, so that we could not be seen if a watcher on the plains had a glass trained on the hill, and we gradually worked our way north where we could command a better view of the pass through the Quiraing and the road along the bay to the Lodge. We settled down behind a rocky pinnacle, where the hill fell sheer for hundreds of feet, as if it had been cleft clean by a giant axe, and the whole wide sweep of the bay was spread below.

The air was that sharp and clear I could make out every hollow in the hill, every corrie and sharp-ridged pinnacle falling to the brown moor, glowing fresh, and the green of the crofts, where the black dots of the grazing cattle were visible for miles around.

About midday, a long, long line of marines wound down through the pass, led by an officer mounted on a pony. Their white forage caps and scarlet tunics made a flowing coloured ribbon down the hill. The column seemed to be never ending. "Mr. Drummond spoke true, Lachlann," I said, "there are hundreds o' them on the march."

Lachlann Ban made no answer. His gaze was fixed on the bay. A fishing smack was nosing into the channel between the island and the shore; a broad beamed craft, high in the bow, her stern too square for my liking, giving her a clumsy line. She dropped anchor in mid-channel, lifting slow on the swell, and swinging idly with the tide.

Lachlann Ban gripped my arm in a fierce clutch. "Sheriff Ivory cannot march his men on water," he exulted. "We are delivered from him, boy. I would know that boat supposing I was blind of an eye. Calum Og is come!"

It was dusk when Lachlann Ban left the cave, and he had not been gone an hour when the first nagging doubts took a hold of me, burrowing like maggots deep in my mind. I was not the only one. As the hours passed, Eachunn Ruadh and Iain Beag grew more and more restless, first one and then the other making off down the narrow passage in the rock to the ledge outside, not saying a word, but their faces a poor mask for their thoughts when they came back in.

My eyes were heavy with sleep, and it seemed to me that dawn could not be far off, he had been gone that long, when Eachunn Ruadh suddenly said, "I doubt he has come to grief."

"Not Lachlann Ban," Iain Beag said, but there was no conviction in his voice.

"Supposing he was wrong about the boat," I said, "and it was not Calum Og at all?"

"Ach, I have known that man tell me whose mark was on a sheep when I was still scouring the hill for a sight o' the beast," Iain Beag said.

"Aye, but he has not got eyes in the back of his head," Eachunn Ruadh said, "and the man was not born that could not be taken from behind. We should never have let him make off on his own. Better any one of us was taken than Lachlann Ban."

"Better none of us," said a voice from the end of the cavern—and there he was, straw-coloured hair plastered over his brow, no trace of tiredness on that eager, laughing face. He was not made for a quiet life, that was a sure thing; he thrived on peril, as blithe to greet it as a drunkard is eager to seize a jug of whisky.

He came forward to the fire, his step as quick and light as if he had newly risen from a long rest. A baggy fisherman's jersey hung down about his thighs. "Calum Og's," he said, fingering the jersey. "I had to swim to the boat."

"What kept you?" Eachunn Ruadh said. "We were after thinking you had come to grief."

"You were not far out," Lachlann Ban said wryly. "I was making round the back o' your byre, Eachunn, when I very near walked slap into a patrol. Six marines, gathered out o' the wind, taking a quiet smoke."

"*Dhia*, you were not for going to the house!"

"Aye, I wanted a word with my chief lieutenant before we made off."

Eachunn Ruadh's brow furrowed. "Chief lieutenant?"

"Your brother, Aonghas."

"You risked going to the house for idle chat wi' a boy o' twelve!" Eachunn Ruadh exclaimed, a slow flush of anger colouring his cheeks. "That was a piece o' nonsense, Lachlann."

"Well, we will see," Lachlann Ban said mildly. "Right enough there were more patrols on the go than I bargained for, and not all o' them holding up the wall of a byre, smoking. The ground is crawling wi' them between the river and the cliffs. I spent more time flat on my face than up on my feet."

"Is Calum Og going to take us?" I put in.

"Take us?" Lachlann Ban laughed. "He is for joining us and trying his luck in America. When I left Calum Og he was roaring out the Battle Hymn O' the Republic." He took his ease on a bed of heather, hands clasped behind his head, that composed you would have thought we were already safe aboard ship for America. "Calum Og has set sail for Rona," he told us. "He will lie up in Big Harbour through the day, and make over at night. He will be waiting for us once it is good and dark."

"If the patrols are thick on the ground, maybe it would be better for us to split up when we make down to the shore," Iain Beag suggested.

"We stick together," Lachlann Ban said, a smile playing about his lips, as if he was savouring some secret joke, "and watch the ranks o' the marines split before us."

He would not say another word, and he could be stubborn when he liked. There was nothing for it but to settle down to sleep. And sleep was slow in coming.

We all slept late. The greater part of the brief winter day was spent by the time we stirred ourselves. But it was the longest day I had ever known, longer than any mid-summer day, when the sun is still lighting the sky at the hour of midnight.

We took turns at keeping watch, and it was Iain Beag

who rushed in to report that two patrols were searching the hill no more than five hundred feet below. But they never found the route to the cave, and as the red sun dropped behind the hill, and the light bled from the sky, they started down to the plain.

There was a full quarter-moon shining bright in the sky when Lachlann Ban led the way out of the cave. The crags were dappled in light and shade. Every pit of shadow was full of lurking menace to my anxious eyes; every slither of falling scree sounding in my ears like the quick feet of our enemies; every dislodged stone another hammer blow on my raw nerves. I could hear the *cailleach's* father, the old *Ceistear*, saying, *Truly, the wicked flee where no man pursueth.*

All that lay between us and the river was a slope of green, broken by rounded knolls, when Lachlann Ban waved us down. We gathered about him, flattened behind a knoll.

"Time to wait," he said softly, scanning the ground from north to south and back from south to north again.

The flames rose first from around the township of Flodigarry in the north, almost every hummock—and there were scores about that township—seeming to spout fire. I looked to the south. Flames were leaping high from the hill that had seen fires lit in olden times, warning of the coming of the Norsemen.

"An awful waste o' peats," Lachlann Ban chuckled, "but boys are always terrible keen on making fires, and Aonghas swore he would get all the boys in every township between Lealt and Kilmaluag on the go."

There was a sudden flurry of bugle calls. Shouted words of command came faint on the air from the other side of the river. We could see the lights of a carriage climbing the north road. There were more bugle calls, and a sudden shrilling of whistles. My heart started to thump as if I was at the end of a run, not the beginning.

And a wild run it was, straight for the cliffs to the point above the sheltered cove, masked from the Lodge by a jutting headland. And I shall never forget Lachlann Ban hurtling down the hidden track to the shore—a track that many a one would never have chanced in broad daylight, let alone by the pale light of the moon—one hand behind him gripping my wrist, boots sliding on scree and rock, face scratched by the whiplash of the branches of stunted alders. I was not believing we were safely down when he released my wrist, and I found myself standing on the shore.

The tide was on the flood, near full. We scrambled over the rocks and crossed a thin crescent of white sand to the jutting headland. We crouched down, waiting, too busy gasping air into our lungs to speak a word, ears strained for the least sound. Across the channel, above the wash of the incoming tide, there sounded the faint creak of rowlocks.

We did not wait for the small boat to ground, but waded out to meet her. Calum Og was at the oars. His golden beard had a silvery sheen in the moonlight, and from the pierced lobe of his right ear there hung a ring of gold. Not a word was spoken, as we piled into the boat. Calum Og bent to the oars, pulling out strongly from the shore. The deeply laden boat rose slow on the swell, glitters of phosphorescent spray sweeping bright over her bows; sparkling like fire off the dripping oars as they broke water.

The smack was riding at anchor in the lee of the island. We scrambled aboard, and we were not slow in raising anchor and hoisting sail. She started to roll as we met the cross-tides at the entrance to the bay, but we were soon out in the open sea, her high prow creaming through the waves.

I stood in the stern, looking back at the dark line of the

towering cliffs, watching the glow of the fiery hillocks; a ring of bright flame about Flodigarry in the north. Soon we were abeam the great beacon that blazed on the hill at Culnacnock, lit in the place where a scatter of moss covered stones was all that remained of the old watch tower. The beacon dwindled terrible swift in our wake. I wondered if it was the last sight I would ever have of that shore; of the *cailleach*, and Seoras and Mairi. Of my father. Most of all, my father.

I was not happy: I was not sad. It was like a dream. The sort of dream that is real enough in every detail; where you can smell the food laid out on the table; feel the heat of the sun on your back; the sting of the hail in your face; recognise the voices speaking in your ear; see the faces passing before your eyes; and still know—deep in some queer, secret corner of your mind—that your senses are playing you false, that it *is* a dream, that you will waken into the old, familiar, everyday world once the dominion of sleep has been broken.

The rest of them were gathered about Calum Og at the helm, laughing and joking and cracking away good style. They were not in any dream, that was a sure thing.

I felt a hand on my shoulder. It was Lachlann Ban. "The boys made a great blaze," he said. "Near every marine in the place must have made off for Flodigarry and Culnacnock. If it is medals that are going, we should have a big one struck for young Aonghas."

"Aonghas?" I said, only half hearing him. "Aye, surely."

He squeezed my shoulder hard. "I believe you are near sleeping, boy."

"Not me," I said. "I was thinking."

"What about?"

"About the *bodach*."

"What about him?"

"It was the night before he got the fever bad. He was talking of a minister he had heard at the big meeting in Portree. Not mocking him at all, but telling what he had to say, in the queer Gaelic the man had. That was before you came back, Lachlann."

"What was he saying, the minister?"

"Ach, something about us not making enough noise. The *bodach* said he was after telling how the walls o' Jericho were laid in the dust by a great noise o' trumpets."

"Well?"

"I was thinking, Lachlann, we laid no walls in the dust. We would ha' been the better of a great noise o' trumpets."

"It is a Joshua you are needing for the like o' that," Lachlann Ban said, "and mind you the same one only put down the walls o' Jericho at the seventh shot. Still an' all, we sounded a trumpet, and I am telling you the blast we made will be heard for many a day to come."

"In America?"

"No, not in America," he admitted, "but we will find many a one there from many a far corner ready to stand fast for their rights. And when the crowd of us come together, boy, maybe you will hear your great noise o' trumpets sounding forth." He smiled, his rare, slow smile, and gave my shoulder a hard squeeze. "Wait you," he said, "it will come to pass. The deaf will have ears and the laggard come running, you may be sure o' that."

I watched him go back to the others, wishing I was of the same mould, and could so easily shed the past and fix my gaze square on what was to come.

Calum Og glanced round at me, the ring of gold in his ear gleaming bright in the moonlight. "Away for'ard,

Alasdair," he called, "and tell that sister o' mine to get brewing tea."

I made my way into the bows, legs braced against the pitching deck, and down the short flight of steps to the galley. She was bent over the stove, her golden hair spilling about her shoulders. "Murdina!" I cried, and stopped, fair tongue-tied.

"They will be wanting tea," she said.

"Aye, they are wanting tea."

"Oh, Alasdair!" She straightened from the stove, and gave a little joyous skip, all pretence of calm gone from her. "It will be good in America, won't it?"

"Aye," I said, waking fresh to the new world, the sound of trumpets strong in my ears, "it will be good, Murdina."

THE END

CATCH A KELPIE

If you enjoyed this book
you would probably enjoy our other Kelpies.

Here's a complete list to choose from: